THE THIRTEENTH KNIGHT

THE THIRTEENTH KNIGHT

Basil Jay

Edward Bear Publishing
Jersey · Douglas · Milton Keynes

THE THIRTEENTH KNIGHT

An Edward Bear Book
Published by Edward Bear Publishing - 1996
A Part of Divisions Four Entertainments Limited
Jersey - England - Isle of Man

Distributed by
Octopus Distribution Limited
P.O. Box 214 - Douglas - Isle of Man
Arnside House, 32 Hutchinson Square, Douglas

Typeset by Avocet Typeset, Brill, Aylesbury, Bucks.

Printed and bound in Great Britain by
Ebenezer Baylis - Worcester

ISBN 1 86 128136 6

To Polly
who patiently read and re-read the manuscript

and

For my daughter Tania who at twelve years old had her own
ideas of how Pimm (who she called Pigdog) should look

Pimm (Pigdog)
drawn by Tania in 1979
when the story was first told.

Win a week-end visit
to a
Medieval Castle

(and take your parents)

Edward Bear is very pleased to be able to offer you a week-end away with your parents, visiting one of the famous old castles of England.

The competition is very simple, all you have to do is tell us the name of the Ninth Knight of Arac.

PLEASE NOW TURN TO THE ENTRY FORM AT THE BACK OF THIS BOOK.

Contents

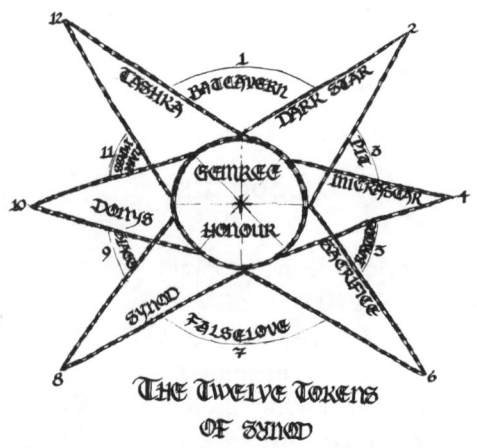

THE TWELVE TOKENS
OF SYNOD

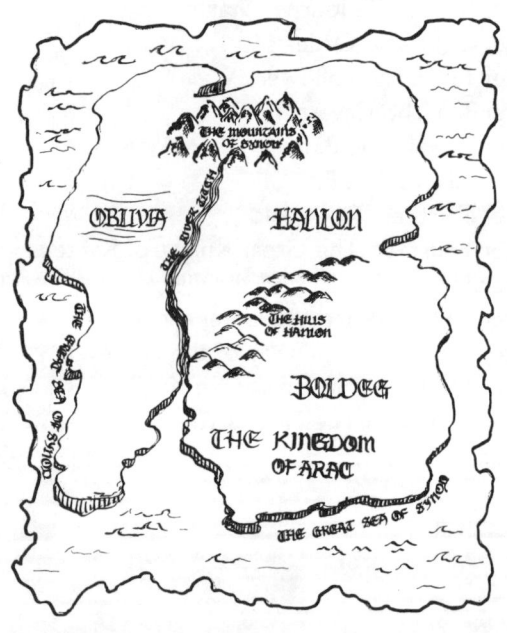

Chapter One

Jeremy Meets Pimm

Pimm was born during the Twelfth Moon of Arac, in the reign of King Pylon V in the land of Boldeg. How Pimm came to be sitting on an up-turned bucket, crying great big Aracican tears into the muddy waters, nobody ever found out (except Jeremy of course – but that was much later).

Jeremy was born on April Fool's Day, and although his mother promised him that that was an accident, it sometimes made him very cross. He was born in the little cottage where he still lived in Grumblehampton with his mother, his father, his brother and his sister. The cottage was very picturesque, and stood almost on the banks of the river. It had a white picket gate that opened onto the towpath at the front, and a rustic stile that led to a flowery meadow, at the back.

Jeremy was twelve years of age, and he was pretty content with life. He got on well with his brother Tim who was eighteen and his sister Tania who was just sixteen (he got on well with his mother and father as well of course, but that doesn't really count). Both his brother and sister were too old now to be interested in adventures,

1

and that meant that Jeremy spent a lot of time on his own.

Luckily, ever since Jeremy had been quite small he had able to escape "at the drop of a hat" his mother used to say, into his imagination. It was true, he could easily slip into his imaginary world where he could be The Crimson Pirate sailing the Spanish Main, The Calico Kid with his six guns slung low on his hips, or best of all, a Knight at King Arthur's court.

"You've not been the same," his mother used to scold him, when she got fed up with his day dreaming, "since you fell in the river and caused that funny little lock-keeper all that trouble." This used to make him cross, because it had happened a long time ago when he was still quite small. He had fallen into the river when he was watching the big barges manoeuvre through the deep and narrow water. Everybody thought he would drown, but the funny little lock-keeper had jumped in and pulled him to safety. When Jeremy had come to, spluttering and spitting out water, the lock-keeper had been so delighted and relieved, that he had given him a curious bronze medallion on a chain. It was a sort of St. Christopher medal, except the picture on it was a small figure carrying an old man across a raging river.

"In future, when you want an adventure," the old lock-keeper had said, "just rub this little fellow, he'll see to it."

Ever since that day, Jeremy found that he always,

usually without thinking, played with the medallion that hung around his neck whenever he was going into one of his 'imaginings'.

Outside his imagination Jeremy was a fairly ordinary twelve year old. He was quite tall, and his blue eyes peeped out beneath a fringe of blond hair that always fell over his forehead and across his eyes. His eyes were – "So big" his Aunt Bessie used to cry, just before she wrapped her great big wobbly arms around him and squeezed so tightly that he could hardly breathe. The only way that he survived Aunt Bessie's 'hello's and 'goodbye's' was by pretending that she was a great big wild grizzly bear in the middle of a frenzied attack, and he was Davy Crockett, the last of the Mountain Men, to whom even grizzly bears eventually succumbed.

Yes, Jeremy was a normal, healthy good looking twelve year old (even though his sister said he had two front teeth that looked like tombstones). He was a boy who, inside or outside his imagination, had a great deal of fun. It was a rare occasion that found him bored or with nothing to do.

Now, that was not quite true, there was just one hour each week when Jeremy got just the teeniest little bit bored. That was on a Sunday afternoon when he had to go to the church hall to Miss Colbran's Sunday School class. It wasn't that he didn't like Miss Colbran, she was good fun, at least she was most of the time when she wasn't being too serious.

It wasn't that he found the stories from the Bible boring. Some of them, like Daniel in the Lions' Den, or Sampson pulling down the Temple, were almost as exciting as the Crimson Pirate. But to have to sit still on a hard chair, in a stuffy old church hall, for a whole hour. He thought this was a waste of a 'no school' day when there were so many exciting things he could be doing.

Jeremy soon discovered that he could make the hour pass much more quickly if he made up 'imaginings' to help things along. Miss Colbran always arranged all the chairs in a sort of half circle for the children. She then sat in the middle where she could see all the children and everybody could see her.

One Sunday Jeremy had been idly playing with the medallion around his neck, when he had gone into one of his 'imaginings'. He was no longer just Jeremy, but Jungle Jem the fearless white hunter. Miss Colbran had ceased to be his Sunday School teacher, she was now the beautiful Jane of the Jungle. She had been tied to a stake in a clearing and a whole tribe of savage pygmies were sitting around her in a semi-circle. Suddenly Jungle Jem noticed that all the pygmies had stood up and were milling about. Jane of the Jungle was calling out angrily and cursing the savages. (Miss Colbran was really saying "thank you children, off you go now, and straight home it will soon be quite dark)." The pygmies (who used to be children) were now converging on Jane of the Jungle (who used to be Miss Colbran) and Jungle Jem knew that he alone could save her. Instinctively he leapt from his hiding place. Squinting across the jungle clearing he spotted a gap in the dense foliage (it was really the door of the church hall). He knew that he had to get help. With a yell he darted for the gap, weaving from one side to the other to avoid the lethal poisonous darts aimed at him from a hundred blow pipes. He knew that once he made the undergrowth he could outrun the savages to the banks of the river. He had hidden his canoe close by, and it was just a few days paddling to the nearest settlement where he could get help. Just as he reached the gap and was about to leap into its comforting protection, the strangest thing happened. Jane of the Jungle called out to him "Bye Jeremy, I'll see you next week". Suddenly Jeremy was back in the church hall again in boring old Grumblehampton. "Bye Miss Colbran" he said sheepishly, and walked out into the autumn sunshine.

Although the sun was shining, it was weak and watery, the sort you only get on winter days, and it was really quite cold. Despite having to go to Sunday School, Jeremy really quite liked winter Sundays. After Sunday School, he would walk home along the river bank. Here he could easily have at least three or four imaginings. Then, when he got home his mother would always say the same thing as he walked through the door, "You're home early dear". It wouldn't matter whether he was early or late or the same time as every other Sunday, she always said the same thing, and then – "take your shoes off and come and sit in front of the fire, the muffins will soon be ready," and that was that. There was always a blazing log fire in the big cottage fireplace. The family would sit around the fire, and toast plate upon plate of hot butter-dripping muffins, in front of the fire. Jeremy loved to use the great long brass toasting fork (which let you get the muffin nice and brown without burning your fingers).

On this particular Sunday, the rude awakening from his Jungle Jem "imagining" and the thought of the blazing fire and the hot muffins was just too much. As he left the church hall he decided he would be just Jeremy and get home as quickly as he could. Taking his hands out of his pockets, he started to jog steadily along the river bank. As he settled into a steady pace, he could hear the crowds that lined each side of the track of the Himalayan Mountain Marathon cheering him on. He knew by now that he was setting a new world record for the toughest road race ever run and that his record would never be beaten. In just two days, he had run through the dangerous mountain section. He had struggled up the side of the famous Mount Annapurna, and was now within sight of Mount Everest, the greatest mountain of them all. He was on the last two miles, and he knew that no one could catch him now. The King of Nepal would be at the finishing line to welcome him and probably make him a Knight or a Lord, or something just as important. Jeremy was getting weaker now, he had been running non-stop for three days.

His legs felt like lead, and his lungs were bursting. He knew the finishing line was very close, and he could hear the crowd shouting, and willing him on.

He could see the famous 'Green Eyed Yellow Idol' (the one in the famous poem) in the distance. From there it was just 100 yards to the finishing line (what he could really see was the haystack by Colley's Bridge, just about 100 yards from where the garden gate of his little cottage opened on to the towpath). As he reached the Green Eyed Yellow Idol, he saw a most remarkable sight. All thoughts of the Himalayan Marathon, the King of Nepal, Knightships, Lordships and cheering crowds went from his mind. There, sitting on an upturned bucket, on the riverbank, just beyond Colley's Bridge was … well it was hard to describe what it was. It was so weird that he thought he must have slipped accidentally into another of his "imaginings". He looked at the river … that looked the same, there was the half -submerged tree that had fallen in after the big storms of the year before last. He looked at Colley's Bridge, which was definitely the same.

Jeremy could see his name, which he had carved into the brickwork when it was the wall of his dungeon, just before he escaped and fought the terrible 'Black Knight'. He looked down at the matching prayer book and bible he was still clutching tightly in his hand. They were the ones that Aunt Bessie had given to him (that was just before she had turned into a wild grizzly bear). Yes, there was no doubt about it. The river was real. The bridge was real. His prayer book and bible were real ... he was real. That meant that the 'person' sitting on the upturned bucket on the banks of the River Titchfield, well ... he must be real too. Jeremy plucked up all his courage, and slowly walked towards him.

Pimm, because we know that that was who Jeremy was looking at, was quite unaware of his presence. He sat very still and stared gloomily into the dark cold waters of the River Titchfield. He was indeed a strange sight as he sat there, his elbows on his knees, rocking slowly backwards and forwards. The first impression was of a little old man – the way his back was bent and his shoulders hunched, the way his little round body rocked. Not so much gently, as wearily backwards and then forwards, backwards and then forwards, just like, Jeremy thought, his own Sailor Gramps.

Sailor Gramps was the name the whole family always called one of Jeremy's grandads so that he was not mixed up with Grandpa Blue Viva. Sailor Gramps had been in the Navy during the war. Grandpa Blue Viva got his name from the little car he had driven around the village since before Jeremy was born. Sailor Gramps was very old and used to sit in front of the fire rocking as if his poor old body was completely worn out and could not sit up straight anymore. Here, however, all resemblance to the old man ended. On top of those scrunched up shoulders (there was hardly any neck that Jeremy could see) was an almost completely round head ... just like a full moon. The head had very neat pointed ears and enormous round eyes. They were a deep shiny black colour (Jeremy could see this even though great big tears kept squeezing themselves out of the corners and running down the pink round cheeks). His nose was like a round button and his mouth reminded Jeremy of a big slice of lemon. It was turned down at the corners at the moment making the face look very sad, but you just knew that when it turned around the other way it would be just the happiest face in the whole wide world.

It has to be said, he presented a very comic figure. He was made even more peculiar by his silver buckled shoes worn over a pair of bright red tights, sort of 'puffed out' short trousers (rather like the ones Sir Francis Drake was wearing in a picture in Jeremy's history book). He had on a silver tunic with an embroidered pattern in the middle of the chest. The pattern appeared to be a large letter A with a sword through the middle of it. However, Jeremy could not see this clearly because the little fellow's arms were in the way. "Ahem!" coughed Jeremy politely "Excuse me, but is there anything wrong?" The little man seemed not to hear. "AHEM!" said Jeremy again, even louder than before, "I said, is there anything the matter?" At this the little face turned around and stared straight at Jeremy. He looked at him with his big black mournful eyes and said sadly. "But everything is the matter. I don't know where I am. I don't know who I am. I don't know where I came from. I don't know where I'm going....and worse of all I don't know how I'm going to get there. Oh" he then added in his strangely deep and tuneful voice ... "and I am really rather hungry."

Now Jeremy felt so sorry for this strange little person, that he blurted out, almost without thinking, and certainly without the slightest thought to what his mother would say ... "You must come home with me and share my muffins". As they walked along together Jeremy turned to his new friend – "What's your name?" he asked. The little fellow said nothing. "Well" said Jeremy "I have to call you something" – he paused, "I know," he finally said, "I will call you Francis Drake."

"What's a muffin?" said Pimm.

Chapter Two

The Knights of Arac

Hills of the north Rejoice
River and mountain spring
Harken the trumpet's voice
Valleys and lowlands sing

Beyond the mountains of Synod, in a land as bleak and stony as its people's hearts, a country prepared for war.

Cannons were cast, swords were fashioned, lances were sharpened. Sodah too had its prophesy, that one day, they would again traverse the secret way through the Guardian Mountains, the secret way to Arac. A prophesy which told them that when that day came Arac would be in chains for ever.

King Pylon V sat on his massive throne in the Great Hall of Synod Castle … the home of the King and the Knights of Arac. The King's throne was set on a dias from which three broad steps led down to twelve ornately carved high back chairs. These handsome chairs were arranged on a lower level in a large semi-circle around the King's throne.

Upon each chair sat a young man. Each wore a

11

suit of silver armour. The sunlight, streaming through the high arched windows of the Great Hall, glanced off the shining metal, adding to the splendour and pageantry of the scene. These young men were the twelve Knights of Arac, (actually only eleven of the chairs were at present occupied, but that will be explained later). Each Knight wore a tabard of silk. Embroidered upon every tabard, each in a different colour, was a large letter A with a sword passing through its centre. This sign was set upon a background shield of the deepest blue. It was the Sacred Sign Of Arac.

By the side of every one of these chairs was an equally ornate stool and upon each stool sat the most remarkable little figure you have ever seen, dressed in silver buckled shoes, over coloured tights and sort of puffed out short trousers. Each in a colour matching that in the Sacred Sign on the tabard of the Knight beside whom they stood. These little fellows were almost comic in their appearance. Their heads were almost perfectly round, with great eyes as black as a mountain pool. Their mouths looked as if they could in one moment be grinning with happiness and in the very next quivering on the edge of tears.

These little men were called 'squires' and they were the servants of their Knights. Not only were they servants to the young Princes, they were also their great and loyal friends. Masters to whose service they had devoted their whole lives and whose colours they proudly wore.

THE KNIGHTS OF ARAC

The Knights of Arac had been summoned this day before King Pylon. He now addressed them.

"My Lords," said King Pylon, "after many hundreds of 'sleeping years', the Prophecy of the True Word is at hand. Our land, the land of Arac that we love so well, is in mortal danger."

Perhaps, before we go on, I should tell you a little about Arac, its history, and the Prophecy of the True Word. Arac is a very ancient country and by far the largest in Highworld. It is now divided into three smaller kingdoms called Boldeg, Hanlon and Oblivia, though it was not always so. Each kingdom is ruled over by a Lord. Each has its own parliament, and even its own language. However, all the people, whether they live in Boldeg, Hanlon or Oblivia, know that above all they are Aracians, people of Arac. It is important to understand just how the countries are arranged geographically and how they came to have their own identities.

To the north of this great land stands a range of mountains. Their peaks are so tall that they thrust their way high above the clouds. The temperature is far below freezing and the mountain tops are always covered with snow and ice. Down in the foothills it is very hot, the ground is rocky and barren and cannot support life. These mountains are called the Guardian Mountains. They separate the land of Arac from the inhospitable and warlike peoples who live in the land of Sodah, beyond the mountains even further to the north. Far down in the south of the land is a great sea. This sea extends from the extreme west to the far east. But more than this, it also runs along the entire length of the western boundary until it reaches the mountains in the north. This sea is so wide that no-one has ever crossed it, and certainly no-one knows whether there are lands beyond it. They call the sea The Great Sea of Synod.

High up in the Guardian Mountains, amongst the snow and ice, a tiny stream begins to flow. By the time it reaches the foothills it is a raging torrent. As it pours across the plains it becomes a mighty river.

This river flows across the fertile plains of Oblivia to join the Great Sea of Synod where the south and the west boundaries meet. The river is known as the River Titch. Finally, there is a range of high hills which run from the eastern-most end of the Guardian Mountains. These form the eastern boundary and then meander across the Plains of Oblivia until they touch the River Titch, which they follow to the Great Sea. Although these hills are not very high, a curious phenomena makes them impassable. For a reason unknown, the Hills of Hanlon, for such is their name, are always covered in a thick and impenetrable mist. So it is that the great country of Arac naturally forms itself into its three Kingdoms. Oblivia, bounded in the north by the Guardian Mountains, in the south and west by the Great Sea of Synod, and to the east the River Titch. Hanlon, sharing with Oblivia the Guardian Mountains to the north and the River Titch to the west, has its southern and eastern boundaries formed by the Hills of Hanlon. And finally Boldeg, the, safest and most protected of all the kingdoms. Protected by the Hills of Hanlon in the north and west, and the Great Sea of Synod in the south and east. Boldeg, the home of King Pylon V, King of all Arac, and of the Twelve Princes who feature in our story.

The story of Arac is not only very important but also very exciting, a story of battles and kitchen boys, of courage and bravery. It is a story that starts many hundreds of years ago, when Arac was quite different from how it is today, when it was not just three kingdoms, but many. There were Ercol and Pramsil, Frigo and Mirando, Charcon and Setas, Dorado, Altesc and many more.

Each of these kingdoms, though small, was perfectly happy minding its own affairs. Except that is for one. Charcon, the country where Hanlon is today. It was the largest, and it was the most secure. Unfortunately Charcon had a greedy and unscrupulous king called King Spitzer. Gradually, over many years, King Spitzer captured kingdom after kingdom until all had succumbed to his armies and he became the most powerful ruler of the Highworld. In each defeated kingdom, where he had survived the fierce fighting, Spitzer banished the beaten king. In his place he sent one of his own Princes to rule on his behalf. To make the administration of his new empire easier (and to save money) he joined many of the kingdoms together . When he had finished there were just three, including his old kingdom of Charcon. He made the Princes charge the people crippling taxes, always far more than they could afford to pay. As the years went by King Spitzer became richer and richer, and the people over whom he ruled became poorer and poorer.

The three young Princes hated what their King was doing. They watched the hardship of the people as they became hungrier with each passing day. They decided to bring the people's suffering to an end, even at the risk of their own lives. First they stopped collecting the taxes. Then they began to divide the land up among the people so that each family could grow its own food and graze its own cattle.

They showed the people how to set up village councils to manage their own affairs, and taught them how to administer the law. They showed them how to contribute to a common purse to pay for the protection of the weak in their communities. But most important of all, they taught the people how to train soldiers to protect themselves from those who would seek to steal from them. Eventually King Spitzer realized that the revenue from his kingdoms had first diminished, and finally ceased completely. He held a council of war and ordered his men at arms to seek out the Princes, to kill them. The men were told to replace them with men loyal to (and perhaps even frightened of) the King. The names of the three young Princes were Boldeg, Hanlon, and Oblivia. It happened, that in the kitchens of King Spitzer's palace there worked a young kitchen boy. His mother and father were tenants of the King's and worked a small farm in the barren foothills of the Guardian Mountains. The land was bad and for several years the crops had failed. Still the King had demanded each year a tax based on the best year of the previous five. This meant that for a long time the boy's parents had been left with barely enough money to feed themselves, the boy and his brothers and sisters. It had been the King's bailiff who had told the boy of the job in the kitchens. There was no pay, just food and shelter for the boy. But the boy knew that with one less mouth to feed his family might survive. He had been just five years old when he was taken to the Palace. That had been seven long years ago, years of back breaking work, from the dawn of each day until long after dusk had fallen. He, more than most, knew of the King's cruelty. Not only had he often experienced severe beatings with little or no cause, but he had watched, time after time, while young men, and sometimes girls, had been flogged unmercifully. These beatings were often for the mildest of misdemeanours, and the King had watched silently from the castle's high windows. One day, the boy was inside the chimney of the huge fireplace cleaning away the deposits of soot caused by the massive kitchen fire. As he worked, he heard two of the palace guards talking.

"The King is furious," said one, "it seems that the three Princes are no longer collecting taxes, they are actually helping the people."

"Yes," said the other, "he is sending his men at arms to kill them and to take over." The boy held his breath in case he gave his presence away.

"They say that he is going to double the old taxes to make up for what he has lost." The first man laughed.

"Boldeg, Hanlon and Oblivia will certainly not die heroes when the people learn of the hardship that their actions have brought upon them."

Their voices died away as they moved slowly out of earshot. Late that same night, the boy packed some food and water. Taking his bag he slung it over his shoulder and set out on the long and dangerous journey through the Guardian Mountains. He had no idea of the dangers ahead, he simply knew that he must warn the three Princes.

That small boy's name was Synod, and his journey is now part of legend, part of Arac's history. Thanks to his warning, the Princes Boldeg, Hanlon and Oblivia successfully fought and beat King Spitzer. Arac was divided into the three kingdoms that we know today and eventually, Synod became the greatest King that Arac had ever known. But that was after the Oblivion. For some years after the wars with King Spitzer the Princes reigned in peace and their Kingdoms prospered. Because of the friendship between them there was no need for armies. The soldiers went back to the fields, and all the weapons were melted down to make ploughs, scythes, and other machinery. Life in Arac was good.

It was then that they came from the land beyond the mountain, a land that, until that time, nobody knew even existed. That was the time of the Oblivion. Arac fought bravely. It retrained the soldiers it had thought it would never need again. It melted down the ploughs and the scythes to mould them again into cannons, swords, and other weapons of destruction. The men, the women and even the children fought bravely for the countries and for the Princes they loved. Though their hearts were full of courage they were no match for the warlike hoards of Sodah, for such was the name of the land beyond the mountains. Soon their countries were overrun. Their beloved Princes, Boldeg, Hanlon and Oblivia were dead, and once again, the people were without hope, just as they had been under the oppression of King Spitzer. Out of this despair there came a hero, once a mere kitchen boy in the castle of the tyrant King Spitzer. Synod was now a Captain in the new army of Arac. He recognised that militarily his armies had no hope against the mighty hoards of Sodah. He knew there must be another way, and he drew upon some strange knowledge that he could feel in his heart although he could not account for it.

Synod's first journey into the Guardian Mountains (his second was when he was a very old man) is now the very stuff of the Legend of

Arac. When all hope was gone, the young man, still not eighteen years old, travelled for many days and nights up into the mountains. He searched for, and found the base camp of the Sodahian King Orcam. There in the heart of the enemy's camp, he challenged the warrior king to meet him in a single handed and one-sided combat. His terms were simple and attractive to the King. If he, Synod, was beaten all his armies would surrender to Orcam. He could end his campaign and return through the mountains to Sodah. All the income and revenues of Arac would be his. But if the King should lose, then he would withdraw his armies and return to his. own land, never to return during his lifetime. Why this great and powerful King accepted a challenge with such odds is not known, perhaps he had too much confidence or perhaps too much pride. Men who were there spoke of a fight that lasted through one day and halfway into the next night. They spoke of the great strength of Orcam, and of the speed and the agility of Synod. The people of Arac never learned of this great fight from the lips of Synod. Never, throughout his long life did he speak of it. It was enough for his people to know that King Orcam, that terrible and mighty King, suddenly and miraculously called his armies out of the land of Arac. However, it did not go unnoticed that their going followed closely upon Synod's long absence into the mountains. Slowly, over many years, small parts of the story of this, battle became known, or guessed at. Songs were sung of it. Plays were acted about it. Still Synod, now a great hero, remained silent as if nursing some secret knowledge. There was a secret to the solving of which Synod had devoted his whole life. When Orcam had been defeated his anger knew no bounds, and yet as a Knight he had no choice but to honour his bargain. But before he left for his journey back through the mountains, he told Synod that although he would never invade Arac during his lifetime, he would devote his life to preparing his sons for its conquest. One day, within a short span of his death, the armies of Sodah would return through the secret mountain way. When that day came Arac would be left a barren wilderness. This was Orcam's pledge. This was the message of King Orcam. The people of Arac proclaimed young Captain Synod King and for many years he reigned.

They were uneasy years, the King, the threat of Orcam never out of his head, built vast defences and trained mighty armies, always waiting for the attack he knew would come. He sent many brave men to try to find the secret way through the Guardian Mountains, the way, the only way through which the invaders could come. Few returned, and of those that did, none had found a way. He sent many brave sea captains in great ships, to try to navigate the great sea to the lands beyond ... if lands there were. Most perished, but those who did not reported that the seas were unnavigable. Near the end of Synod's reign, and now a very old man, he gathered together the

THE THIRTEENTH KNIGHT

reports of his sea captains. He gathered together the reports of all the brave young men who had tried to find a way through the mountains. With these, and these alone, he set off to find the secret way and to fulfil the destiny he knew was his. Synod was gone for more than twelve years.

The people believed that he had perished. Then, one day a tired and weary old man arrived at the castle of the long lamented King. His back was bent, his hands were clenched and gnarled. His hair was snow white and like his long and matted beard, reached nearly to his waist. But the eyes of this old man were shining and triumphant. King Synod had returned, and for many days the people of Arac celebrated a miracle. The King called around him his closest advisors and told them his remarkable story. He had spent three years in a small boat, armed only with the reports of his captains. He had sailed for many months at a time, living off fish he caught each day, and drinking water from the sea. His audience had gasped at this, knowing as they did that drinking sea water turned people mad. The king smiled. "You see," he had said, "the Great Sea, as we have always called it, is not a sea at all, but a huge inland lake. It is larger than the mightiest sea, and is fresh water. I sailed through storms that turned the waters into mountains. Through winds that howled like banshees, and yet, providence was on my side. I survived to land on a friendly shore. The land was called Patos. The people were kind and peace loving. They knew not of the land of Sodah, nor indeed of Arac. I stayed for one full year, but then, leaving them on their guard I sailed along their western coast. I approached the Guardian Mountains at the point where they first begin to rise out of the northern most deserts."

The King then told them how for six years he had traced and retraced the steps of every young man who had reported to him. But there was nothing. And then, when his resolve was almost at its end, he had wandered into a cave to rest. There had been a mighty storm while he had slept. He had woken to find that the rains had formed a fierce river of water that rushed along the crevice below the ledge on which he stood. Strangely the river flowed swiftly into the deep darkness of the cave, and yet the water level did not rise. In that moment King Synod realised that he had found the secret way.

The King followed the river for many days and nights, deeper and deeper into the very heart of the mountains.

There were places where the roof of the caves was so low that he had to crawl on hands and knees. There were places where the roof was so high and the walls so wide that he could have been on the open mountain side. He knew by the deep impenetrable darkness that his was not so. He came to know size only by the way his shouts echoed and bounced off the damp cold walls. After many weeks, King Synod at last passed out of the secret way and into the dreaded land of Sodah. The entrance to the secret way from the

Sodahnian side appeared at the bottom of a deep pit. It was impossible to find it by accident and Synod was most careful to mark his way in readiness for his return. Wearing various disguises King Synod spent three years wandering that bleak land. During his wanderings he learned the reason that the people of Sodah had not returned to wreak their vengeance upon Arac. The secret way that had taken King Synod and his brave captains so long to find, had been discovered by King Orcam, the King that Synod had fought, and apparently mortally wounded. Orcam had been true to his word to Synod, and, following his defeat had set off back through the secret way with his armies. The way was, as Synod now knew, long and difficult, and the King had soon died of his wounds. His armies had struggled on, but all but a handful of men had been struck down by a strange illness and did not reach the journey's end. Those who made it to the bottom of the pit failed to find their way out. Its secret, upon which Synod had stumbled by pure luck, had died with their King. And so, the great army of Sodah had perished. The secret way had died with them and, until such a time as the secret was re-discovered, Arac would remain safe. In his last days, Synod called to his bedside the twelve bravest young men in the land. To each he gave a silver box and a 'Word'. The Word was the key to open the box, and inside this box lay a 'Token'. Only when all the Tokens were laid together would the secret way be unlocked.

Synod dubbed these twelve Princes, the Knights of Arac. He told them that their destiny, and that of their son's, and their son's sons, was to guard the secret of the mountain way – the 'True Word'. When the time was right, and they would know when that time was, they would gather at the appointed place . Then, their Tokens would be joined and their secret Word spoken. Only then would the secret way be sealed forever. The Tokens were then taken back by Synod for keeping by 'another' until the time was revealed. That 'other' yet unknown, would come to them and be known and recognised as The Thirteenth Knight.

When King Synod died there was much

sadness throughout the land. They called the mighty lake 'The Great Sea Of Synod'. They called the Guardian Mountains, 'The Mountains of Synod' and they all prayed that the time of the True Word would not happen in their lifetimes.

And so it was to be. Many Kings followed Synod. Many young Princes took their vows as the Knights of Arac. As son followed father through the generations the destinies of the Knights became distant and vague. King Synod, Prince Boldeg, Hanlon and Oblivia took their rightful places first in history and then in legend, and the True Word became a prophecy for the future.

Chapter Three

The Visions

"Knights of Arac" began King Pylon, looking around the half circle of young men, each attended by his squire.

"You have all returned from your vigil on the Mountains of Synod." The King paused and looked at the earnest young Princes seated before him with their eager and trusting squires beside them. "While you have been away we have all come to know that the time of the Prophesy of the True Word is at hand. The Prophesy that will make our beloved land safe and peaceful for all time." The King turned his gaze upon the young Prince who occupied the first chair. A tall fair young man who wore a tabard of white with the Sacred Sign of Arac emblazoned upon the deep blue of the shield. "Prince Edmund, First Knight of Arac, tell us your story."

The young man rose. He unsheathed his sword, and turning, placed it in the waiting hands of his squire. This was the tradition when a Knight was to approach his King. He turned back towards the Throne and mounting the steps, knelt before King Pylon.

"Sire," he began, "my squire and I travelled for many weeks through the Guardian Mountains. We crossed the plains of Oblivia, and made our way to our station. Each Knight had an area of the land of Boldeg to patrol. This territory was called his 'Station'". "On our journey there were many strange happenings. It soon became clear that this would be no ordinary tour of duty." Edmund looked up into the King's face and the King motioned him to continue. "But none was as strange as that series of events which overtook us high in the mountains of Synod, when we were but a few day's journey from our destination." Here Edmund paused, and remained silent for some minutes, as if thinking deeply. At last the King laid his hand upon the Prince's shoulder and whispered softly "Go on my boy, tell us your story."

"The night was bitterly cold." Edmund spoke, as if to himself. "Snow had been falling for many hours. My squire and I were well clad in garments of fur, yet still the cold penetrated to our very bones." If anybody had been looking they would have seen Prince Edmund's squire, Etum, wrap his arms tightly around his pudgy little body and shiver violently. But no-one was looking. All eyes were staring fixedly at Edmund, hanging on his every word. He continued. "We had fashioned a crude shelter between two huge boulders. This served to keep out the cruel wind and give us a little comfort. Eventually my squire fell into a deep and unnatural sleep, as if nothing in this world would ever awaken him." Edmund turned and looked towards his squire, as if to check that he was indeed still with him.

"Though he slept deeply, he slept without any distress or discomfort. His skin, which moments before had, like mine, been blue with the cold, now glowed with the bloom of warmth and health. Whatever it was that had given him such comfort, I envied him as I sat through those dark, cold hours praying that sleep would be offered to me." Again Edmund stopped speaking. This time the Great Hall remained quiet, no-one dared to break the spell by prompting the young Prince. After some minutes of silence he began to speak once more.

"Eventually I slept, but it was a nightmarish sleep. I was tormented by strange and terrible dreams, and then, suddenly, I was awake. I became aware of a bright and dazzling light. It seemed to bathe the whole area in warmth and calm – even the wind no longer howled." Edmund looked silently into the middle distance. The King made no attempt to restrain himself. Leaning forward he touched the young man's arm. "Please go on," he said. Edmund resumed his story, but now so quietly that the Knights had to strain to hear the words.

"I left my bed of skins and went out into the night. I knew not where I was going, or why. I just had this compulsion to move towards the light. My squire was still sleeping soundly, and with great peace. The light seemed to beckon me on, and I followed beneath snow laden trees. I crossed frozen streams and passed along rock strewn paths. Although the way was rough and the mountain track steep and slippery, not once did I stumble or fall. At last I came to a large clearing where the snow was as clean and unmarked as the ermine on a King's cloak, a carpet of the purest white with not a blemish disturbing its beauty. There, in the centre of the clearing, where the footprint of neither man nor beast broke the surface, stood an old man, an old man with long flowing hair and a beard as white as the snow beneath his feet. Yet this was no fragile old man. Here was no bent back or thin undernourished body. His face spoke of great age, and yet the way he held himself, his posture, his presence was that of a warrior. In his hand he held a broadsword that made my own war-sword appear as no more than a whittling knife. The blade of this huge sword glowed like fire. Indeed, it was the sword that was the source of the great and warming light that had beckoned me forth." Again Edmund stopped speaking and this time the silence was spellbinding. When he continued, his voice seemed even lower than before, his face coloured with modesty as he related the old man's words.

"Edmund, First of the Knights of Arac," the old man's voice had boomed in his head, and yet no sound seemed to come from his lips. "I have watched you through your years of Knighthood. You have done well, a truly brave and chivalrous knight. Your courage has been, and is, beyond question. I come to you now because your greatest courage is yet to be called upon. The time of the True Word draws nigh. You must go back now in haste, back to Boldeg, back to your King. Take with you this Token. It will play its part in revealing the secret way that forms the essence of the True Words Prophecy. Remember the word that I will now entrust to you. Even now your enemies, our enemies, gather and time runs short – so prepare, the prophecy will be fulfilled. Your token is 'Jet', your word is 'Cavern'. Go now and report to your King." Edmund looked straight into the melancholy eyes of King Pylon. He put his hand into the leather pouch around his waist. Withdrawing his hand, he brought forth a half-circle of strange stone, triangular in shape and as black as jet. "I do not remember the journey back to my shelter and my squire. I remember only waking, long after dawn had broken. I felt warm and rested, the memory was still vivid in my mind, and lest I doubted its happening, I was clutching this Token firmly in my hand." Edmund stopped speaking and silently bowed his head.

"Thank you Prince Edmund, brave Knight" said King Pylon. Edmund stood, bowed to his King and returned to his chair. Etum rushed forward and proudly returned Edmund's sword. The young

Prince slipped it into its sheath and resumed his seat.

One by one the King called the other Knights to tell their own stories.

Prince Fanon the second Knight of Arac. Prince Ogam, the third Knight. Prince Hanno, the fourth. The Princes Retne, Smadra and Tevdu, the fifth, sixth and seventh Knights. Prince Erac, the eighth and Prince Luan the ninth. Finally came The Princes Mala and Fion, the tenth and eleventh Knights. All had similar tales to tell. All, in their own stations, had met the old man with the long white beard and flaming sword. All had been given a Token and a Word. All had been told to return in haste to their King and to prepare for the True Word.

"My Princes" said the King when all the stories had been told, "Only you hold the Tokens to open the secret way. Only you have been told the Word. King Pylon looked steadily around the Great Hall. "However, I alone hold the Prophecy of the True Word that will guide us to the place where the Tokens will be joined." King Pylon stopped and frowned as if trying to remember a difficult problem. "The Prophecy is in six parts: The Visions, The Dream, The Ordeal, The Follower, The Sacrifice and The Thirteenth Knight. Until all the parts have been revealed to me the whole prophecy cannot be completed and the Tokens cannot be joined." The King paused and thought deeply. "Until the Tokens are joined, the secret way will remain open to our enemies."

"My Lord," interrupted Prince Fion, "what did our adventures mean, were they the Visions of which you speak?"

"They were indeed the Visions, my Prince," returned the King, "the warning given to us that our enemies have re-discovered the secret way from Sodah to Arac. The warning that, even now, they prepare for war. You, each of you, have fulfilled the first part of the Prophecy. You have spoken to King Synod. You have been given the Word and the Token that will play the final role in the prophecy. Guard them both well."

"My King"

"Yes Prince Edmund," replied King Pylon.

"Now that the Visions have been revealed to you, what does the second part of the prophecy, The Dream, signify?" The King stood up from the throne and walked slowly around the half circle of Knights looking each firmly in the eye before replying.

"The Prophecy says that there would be twelve Visions before the dream. Before the dream can be revealed to me I must know the twelve Tokens, and the twelve Words. I must know each of the twelve Visions. King Pylon now stood before the empty chair of the twelfth Knight. He turned and sat down. Pimm, the squire to the twelfth Knight of Arac, squire to the Prince Gemree, sat quietly upon the stool by the side of his masters chair, the chair now occupied by the great King Pylon. His gaze was fixed firmly upon his silver buckled shoes. He felt the King's hand rest upon his shoulder and heard his soft and kindly voice say, "I know but eleven Visions." He paused, "Prince Gemree has not returned."

Chapter Four

Pimm Remembers

Isles of the southern seas
Deep in your coral caves
Hark to the warring breeze
Rise now your restless waves

The hot, dusty plain, which had been empty just short hours before, gradually filled, as line upon line of men marched, in battle formation, out of the great walled city of Sodah to take their places in the growing army.

Shields and lances clanged musically together, and breastplates of steel glinted in the sun. The murmur of voices was like the restless swell of the sea beneath the storm sounds of the heralds' trumpets. Soon Arac would be no more.

Francis Drake sat on an upturned bucket on the banks of the River Titchfield eating a cold muffin. It was the same bucket that he had sat on almost six months ago when he had first met Jeremy – (it was a different muffin of course).

It seemed to Francis Drake that all he ever ate these days was muffins. He reckoned that he must have eaten at least a million muffins since that first winter's Sunday afternoon. Francis Drake thought back with an amused smile, a smile that completely transformed his round, moon-like face, until it looked just like the 'smiley' face on Jeremy's jeans.

"Hello mum," Jeremy had said as he had walked into the room where the family were just settling down in front of the roaring fire. There was a large plate with funny white things on it. These they were sticking on the end of a long brass fork and holding them in front of the fire. "Can you do some extra for my friend?" Jeremy's mother had looked up and given a little scream of surprise. The rest of the family had just sat open mouthed and speechless with amazement.

"What, what's your new friend's name?" his mother had stammered.

"He doesn't know," Jeremy had replied, "so I'm going to call him Francis Drake."

Well, since that blackened lump that had been his first muffin (Jeremy's mother had been so taken aback that she had quite forgotten that she had been holding the toasting fork in the fire), he had eaten hot muffins, cold muffins, muffins with jam, muffins with honey – once when Jeremy and his mother were out shopping, he had even tried to make muffin soup, but that really hadn't worked out very well at all.

Jeremy's family had soon come to accept Pimm's strange presence. Pimm (or Francis as he was now called – the family had soon got tired of the Drake bit) was always very polite. He always used his handkerchief He never (or hardly ever) sniffed and he always said 'bless you' when anyone sneezed. He tried very hard not to be any trouble, and he made no demands at all (other than for a plentiful supply of muffins).

They made him up a very comfortable bed in an old wardrobe, which they laid on its side close to the big old boiler in the garage. It was filled with blankets and pillows and, all things considered, he was pretty contented.

He still used to get this strange feeling, from time to time, that there was something important that he had to do. Occasionally, he would look curiously at Jeremy. Something about his blue eyes, or the way his blond fringe flopped over his forehead, would stir a distant memory in his mind. Then in a flash it would be gone and he would get on with the far more important business of thinking about his next plate of muffins.

When Pimm had first moved in with Jeremy's family, life had been very odd. For several weeks there had been non-stop processions of people calling on all sorts of strange pretexts. Boy Scouts, wanting to do Bob-a-Job jobs when it wasn't even Bob-a-Job week. Girls wanting to do some shopping for Jeremy's mother, or to take the family's dog for a walk. Old Ladies coming to collect for some old bazaar or 'sale of work'. What they really wanted of course, was a chance to see this strange little man called Francis Drake. The strange little person absolutely everybody in the village was talking about. But soon people just got used to seeing him in his funny little costume. Gradually they took less and less notice until, eventually, they didn't seem to notice him at all.

Pimm got up and stretched his legs. He began to walk slowly up and down the river bank. After a while he left the river and started to walk across the meadow towards the woods. He knew that although he was walking away from the river, he would meet up with it again. At this point, it flowed in a great big circle, and doubled back on itself, re-appearing on the other side of the wood. Somehow, Pimm knew that it was important to stay close to the river, something told him that it was to play a very important part in his future. All day long, the feeling that he sometimes had, that there was something important that he had to do, had been stronger than ever. Odd visions kept flashing through his mind. He saw some big iron gates, and then the image of a beautiful waterfall with a rainbow passing through it. In the meadow a black horse was quietly grazing. As Pimm passed by he looked up lazily and Pimm found himself looking into the horse's eyes. Just for a moment he nearly had it. Like when a word is on the 'tip of your tongue', but you can't quite make it come out. So it was with Pimm, "Black horse, black horse, black horse," he kept muttering to himself as he screwed his eyes up trying to think. It was no good – none of it made any sense.

He had spent a troubled night in his wardrobe in the garage. A night of meaningless dreams. He had seen knights in shining armour. He had seen old men with long white beards, he had seen black horses by the thousand, and beautiful maidens. Poor Pimm awoke before it was properly light. He felt very confused. Still, looking on the bright side he thought, today is Sunday. He quite liked Sundays because on a Sunday afternoon Jeremy went to Sunday School. This gave him a whole hour to do just what he wanted to do while he was waiting outside the church hall for Jeremy to come out. He was therefore a little surprised when Jeremy's mother said "Francis, why don't you go to Sunday School with Jeremy today, I have had a word with Miss Colbran, and she will be delighted to see you."

Now Pimm was absolutely thrilled to bits with the idea and could hardly wait for the hands of the clock to reach 3 o'clock so that he could walk through the doors of the church hall for the very first time.

"Hello," said Miss Colbran with a great big smile, "you must be Jeremy's friend, Francis Drake – do come in and sit in that chair". She pointed at the chair at the very end of the half circle of those arranged to face her.

Pimm suddenly stepped backwards with a start, his mind racing back to another time and another place. He could see twelve ornate chairs arranged in a semi-circle around a huge throne. He could see twelve young men in silver armour (one of them looked remarkably like Jeremy). He stared up at Miss Colbran in her tweed skirt and cardigan and her sensible shoes. He saw a tall majestic figure in a fur trimmed cloak and golden crown. Pimm bowed low. "Thank you King Pylon" he said. All the children laughed and so did Miss Colbran. "My, you are a funny little person" she chuckled.

Chapter Five

The Twelfth Vision

King Pylon looked down kindly on Pimm who stood before him with head bowed. "Pimm," he said gently, "you are the squire and friend to Prince Gemree, twelfth Knight of Arac, you set out with our prince, but you returned alone. Tell us your Master's story."

Pimm looked up into the kind, tired eyes of King Pylon. "I will try your Majesty" he said quietly, and this is the strange tale he had to tell.

"It was early morning" Pimm began, "when my Lord and I set out from this castle for his station in the mountains of Synod. My Lord's station, as you know Sire, is high in the mountains close to the source of the River Titch. We travelled through the foothills of the Guardian Mountains. It is a route that we know well and one that has never offered us dangers on our past journeys." Here Pimm, warming to his story, paused, and looked around the Great Hall at the eleven Knights and their squires. Twenty-three pairs of eyes were fixed unwaveringly upon him.

"My Lord Gemree was uneasy almost from the first day" Pimm went on, "He kept looking behind him as if fearful that someone was following. For three long days and three longer nights we travelled in this fashion. At last, as the sun set to bring to a close the third day, Prince Gemree could bear it no longer. We made camp, and he told me to light a huge fire and to keep it burning brightly until he returned. I did as he said, and for ten days and nights I kept the fire piled high with brushwood from the nearby forests. The flames leapt and danced tirelessly as each new day followed each night.

As the sun began to set on the eleventh day I heard the sound of hooves moving through the thick scrub on the mountain slopes below me. I feared the worst, and was greatly relieved when my Lord Gemree appeared, and rode into the firelight."

Pimm stopped talking and looked pensively at the floor.

"Go on" the King prompted him.

"Yes sire," said Pimm, and resumed his tale. "In the glow of the firelight I saw my master's face, It was the same, and yet it was different. There was a smile on his lips as if at some inner thought. His eyes were bright and shining and his face seemed somehow soft and gentle. He looked at me and said, "Pimm, my loyal squire and true friend, I have seen wonderful things, I have heard wondrous words. I have met my destiny. We have much to do, you and I, and we will be tested to the full. Pimm," his eyes shone and his face was earnest, "we will not be found wanting, for what we do now we do for our beloved Arac." At this point, Edmund, the First Knight of Arac, could contain himself no longer. "Pimm" he cried out, "good squire to my dear friend the Lord Gemree, tell us where he is, is he safe? will he be …?"

"Edmund" King Pylon held up his hand and motioned the agitated Knight to silence. "Be patient, let the good squire finish his story." Pimm looked at Prince Edmund.

"Lord Gemree explained nothing, he simply bade me collect our things, put out the fire and prepare to continue our journey. For many days and nights he did not eat or sleep, yet he was always most anxious for my welfare. During this time he seemed to know neither tiredness nor hunger. When we stopped, which we did from time to time so that I could rest, my Lord sat straight backed upon his horse, unmoving, looking upwards towards the course of the moon and holding his sword firmly in his hands. Always upon his face in these days was an expression of great contentment, even pure joy."

The King moved away from Pimm, and mounted the steps that led to the great throne. He sat, and leaned towards the little squire. Pimm waited until he had settled and then continued.

"We came to the River Titch at the point where the Guardian Mountains, the Forests of Hanlon, and the Plains of Oblivia meet. There we turned northwards to follow the river to its source. The way was difficult, but the journey was uninterrupted and we reached our destination just as the moon entered its last quarter." Pimm stopped and stood quietly with his eyes cast down. This time no-one spoke and after a short while he began speaking again. "At last, my Lord took both food and drink, and then he slept. We had camped in a clearing close to where the river rose as a deep black pool hundreds of feet above us. Across the clearing were two huge boulders that marked the point where the river ended its plunge from the craggy cliff tops. The waterfall formed by this phenomena must be one of the greatest sights in Arac. The water hits the boulders with such force that spray leaps into the air as though the river itself is trying to fly back to its source. In front of the foot of these great falls is a large flat rock that men call the Tablestone. It was upon this stone that my Master rested and where for many days he slept a deep sleep from which nothing could awaken him.

On the eleventh day he awoke and looked at me." Pimm looked straight up at the shaft of sunlight that pierced the room from the high, arched windows. "My master left the Tablestone, upon which water cascaded in waves, and came and stood before me. His garments were as dry and crisp as if he had spent the day walking in the summer's sun."

"'Pimm' he said to me, 'I must leave you now. I have had a vision denied to all men, a dream so real and wonderful in its clarity that it has marked my destiny forever. Now I must go on, but I must go alone'" There were tears in Pimm's eyes as he remembered that painful parting. He looked at the King.

"Sire" he said, "My master then said – 'Take this token and remember this True Word. You, Pimm, must take my place at the appointed hour. Now, go back to the castle of King Pylon, already my brother Knights and their squires return. Tell his Majesty that I have had a vision, and a dream, and in that dream I met the great King Synod, who told me that I was the chosen Knight, and that I must set out my vision and entrust it to my squire." As he spoke these words Pimm pulled a roll of parchment from his tunic. He approached the King and placed it into his hands. "With these words Sire my Lord Gemree mounted his horse and rode away without looking back."

King Pylon sighed and then smiled. "Thank you Pimm," he said, "you have done well. You have said nought of your journey home but we know that alone, it would have been long and difficult. You have borne it with great courage and fortitude and I, and the Knights of Arac salute you. Now," the King smiled kindly at Pimm, "I must bid you leave us. What must follow can only be learned by those privy to the secret of the Tokens and the Words."

After the twelve squires had left the Great Hall the King turned again to the young men who sat before him. "Knights of Arac," he began, ."you know as well as I the Prophecy of the True Word. I have told you that the Dream would not be revealed until all the Visions had been told. This was true, the prophecy required that the vision be 'told' in our brother Knight's own words. These words, thanks to the courage of a brave little squire, we now have." The King held up the parchment. "With sadness I must tell you of a part of the prophecy I knew, but could not reveal until now. You have heard that Prince Gemree told Pimm that he was the chosen Knight. I can tell you now, that the prophecy decrees that the chosen Knight, Prince Gemree, will not return."

Chapter Six

The Dream

King Pylon read from the parchment of Prince Gemree. "My King," he had written, "a wonderful thing happened to me as I travelled to my station in the Mountains of Synod. I have had a vision. I know that it is important to the future of our land. In my vision I was told that I must write down all that has happened to me since I left our castle, many weeks ago. This I now do, and will instruct my good squire Pimm to journey back to Boldeg with my words." The King looked up, the Knights were unmoving, hanging on his every word.

He continued "As we travelled first across the Hills of Hanlon, through the dark mists. I felt no fear as Pimm and I had made the journey many times and knew our landmarks by heart. We crossed the River Titch at the crossing place and set out over the plains of Oblivia, an easier journey than that through the forests of Hanlon. Still I felt no discomfort. It was as we first started through the foothills of the mountains of Synod that I first began to feel uneasy, as if I was being followed." The King stopped as a Knight coughed softly. He waited for silence before continuing. "This feeling was not one of fear, almost the opposite. I felt as if we were being followed by someone who cared for our safety and was not threatening it.

This strangeness persisted for two days and two nights. During the third night, when the world is at its quietest, a voice within my head told me to turn around and retrace my steps alone. I bade Pimm light a huge fire to protect him from the wolves that roam the lower reaches of the mountains. I told him to keep it piled high and burning day and night until I returned.

With each step a feeling of great contentment settled about me. I just knew that what was going to happen was important. That I would have little control over it, and I knew that I was in no danger. It was in such a frame of mind that eventually, feeling very tired, I stopped and sat down with my back against a huge oak tree. I quickly fell asleep.

While I slept the strangest thing happened. An old man, his white beard almost down to his waist, and a mane of the purest white hair you have ever seen, came to me and told me to wake up. I opened my eyes. This fine old man carried in his hand a flaming sword. Somehow I knew that this was King Synod after whom the mountains themselves were named, and that the sword he held was the sword once wielded in battle by Prince Boldeg.

The old man had held out his hand and helped

me to my feet.

As we stood side by side I glanced back at the oak tree against which I had been sleeping. I started forward at what I saw. Even now I find it hard to write down the words. There, against the oak I sat still, my eyes were closed and I was breathing deeply in a deep and comfortable sleep. The old man smiled and touched my shoulder as I stood beside him".

'My boy' he said, 'there are many things that you will not understand. Let your body sleep and keep its strength for the trials that lie ahead. We have far to go and we will travel faster in spirit'

I did not understand, but I followed gladly. We seemed to float over the land. As we floated over the land below, King Synod told me that I had been chosen from all the Knights of Arac to undertake the Ordeals. Part of the seven acts of the Prophecy of the True Word. An important part without which the secret way could not be closed. He talked in a tongue I understood, but a language that was strange. He said 'do not be afraid, you have much to gain and nought to fear. Your destiny was written long ago. It is through you and you alone that we can find the Thirteenth Knight whom the Prophecy demands. A Knight not of our world, but through him alone can the tokens be joined.'

Below us lay the great junction where the River Titch, the Plains of Oblivia and the Hills of Hanlon met. I was seeing sights that only the eagles see. We turned West and journeyed on.

THE THIRTEENTH KNIGHT

Soon we reached the shores of the Great Sea of Synod. We turned to the North until once more the foothills of the Mountains of Synod lay beneath us. Then upwards, up and up and up, until the ground below us was covered in snow and huge glaciers glinted in the sun. We were floating no more but hovering over a deep lake held in a basin between four mountain peaks."

King Synod again touched my shoulder. 'Brave Knight,' he said in his strange language 'below us lies the very source of the River Titch, it is here that your journey, the journey that you must take alone, will begin.' I turned towards him but he had gone.

Suddenly my head was filled with images. I found myself travelling down faster and faster towards the surface of the black water. Through what magic I do not know, I plunged straight into the pool that was the source of the river. I grabbed a huge lungfull of air, but soon I could hold my breath no longer. My eyes were tightly shut and blackness enveloped me. Reluctantly, and without choice, I took a great breath as my tortured lungs fought for air. I waited for them to fill with water, but instead they filled with sweet fresh air. Cautiously I opened my eyes expecting to see the terror of that deep pool; instead I saw rainbows of beautiful colours. I felt my garments and they were as dry as dry can be. And yet, the sensation I felt was that of sinking slowly and weightlessly through a warm clear pool. I looked around more closely. Around me waterfalls danced, but I found I was falling, or rather floating, between water, not through it. I passed through huge caverns where monstrous bats, with wings like cloaks and eyes like rubies, floated and darted before my eyes. Then the visions changed, and I was falling faster and faster. Now through deep pits, where lizards and snakes writhed and scuttled; where each crack, each crevice gave up a creature that made my heart beat faster and my skin crawl.

Gradually the darkness faded, now I was falling more slowly and then floating once more. Below me now lay fields of corn with high golden ears waving in the sunshine. Now there lay great forests, dense green foliage forming a canopy over the hidden life beneath. Below me now were great rivers, and serene blue lakes. Scenes of the greatest beauty and calm. I saw a most beautiful maiden with fair skin and golden hair as graceful as a swan. She called to me by name but then she was gone.

Slowly the skies darkened and before me now lay a castle, not a place of joy and happiness but of evil and unrest. The castle, with battlements thrusting high into the sky blocked my way forward. Walls as sheer as cliffs rose to either side, and there was no way past. In front of the castle stood a huge black stallion, upon its back a mighty Knight dressed all in black, a giant of a man who wore evil like a cloak. And then this scene too was gone, and sunlit fields lay below . Meadows and flowers carpeted the hills. Now again appeared the beautiful maiden. She held out her arms towards me and I could see that she was calling – but I heard no sound. And now there were gates of iron, huge gates, tall and majestic between two stone pillars that stood thrusting their way upwards. Before the gates stood a wizened figure. He was wearing a green tunic and on his head was a pointed hat with a long feather. He called to me.

"Prince Gemree" he said, "I have been waiting for you. To reach these gates you have proved yourself a brave Knight worthy of unlocking the way to the world that lies beyond. You will have crossed the waterfalls of light, travelled through the caverns of bats and the pit of snakes. You will have met and defeated the Great Knight of Rantoc, and rescued the Maiden of Micrascar. You stand before me now, in a dream. There must come a time when you will strand before me in the real world. If you reach these gates you will have completed a frightful journey. You will have faced and triumphed over the Prophecy's ordeals. And yet, when you reach these gates, your greatest ordeal will still be before you. The Prophecy demands from you reserves of courage upon which no man should be asked to draw. You must open this gate for the one who will follow you. You will open it by an act of supreme and selfless sacrifice, because my Prince, there is only one price that I, the keeper of the gate will accept for the key. That price is your life, not taken, but given by you, given freely, without resistance, and in the name of your King, your country and the Thirteenth Knight."

It was a strange and terrible speech, yet I felt uplifted. Before I could answer, the images began to fade. I do not remember the journey back, only that I awoke again with my eyes heavy with sleep, my limbs cramped and stiff, and my back still supported by the great oak. King Synod stood before me – 'Prince Gemree' he said, 'as I have told you, the Prophecy of the True Word has Seven Parts.

The first of these parts is The Visions, twelve in number and shared by your brother Knights. Through the visions are the twelve Tokens and True Words received.

The second of the parts is the Dream granted to you alone.

The third part is the Journey. This will be undertaken first by you to clear the way for another.

The fourth of the parts is the Ordeals – to be undertaken by you alone.

The fifth part is the Following and that role belongs to another who shall be called The Follower.

The sixth of the parts is the Sacrifice – your sacrifice, Prince Gemree.

And the seventh and final part of the Prophecy is the Thirteenth Knight – we know nought of this except that he will be not from our world.

You Gemree are the Chosen One. You and you alone can open the way for the Follower, you and you alone can fulfil the prophecy for the Thirteenth Knight. Go back now to your squire, set down your vision and your dream and bid your squire take it, in haste, to your King. For you Gemree there can be no return, Prepare the way now for he who must follow.'"

King Pylon laid aside the parchment, he looked up and spoke to the young princes. "Please leave me now, brother Knights" he said.

"I grow tired, and I must prepare for the next part of the prophecy – return to me when the moon is in the eastern sky."

King Pylon slept, his sleep was deep but troubled. When he awoke his face was lined with worry and sadness. Although it was not yet time, he rang the great bell that summoned his Knights. He also called his squire and told him to inform his court that he would have them attend on him in the Great Hall. Then he leaned back wearily and waited.

The low murmur of voices rose and fell as the Great Hall slowly filled. Only the Knights and the King sat silently waiting. At last, when the room had settled, the King spoke. "My subjects," he began, "the time has come for me to tell you of a secret that my Knights and I have borne for many months." He paused, "the Prophecy of the True Word is about to be fulfilled."

An excited buzz filled the Great Hall as the people turned to each other talking animatedly, their eyes bright with alarm. Gradually the noise lessened, and then silence fell as the people turned to face the King.

"Arac faces its Armageddon" he said, "but Arac

can be saved." The King paused and looked from face to face. It was as though time had stopped. Not a soul in the room moved.

"The Prophecy of the True Word is part of our legend, part of our history. As babies we are told it at our mother's knee, as children we are taught it in our schools. There is not a man woman or child in our land who does not know the wickedness of King Spitzer, who does not know of the goodness of the three Princes Boldeg, Hanlon and Oblivia, and the great courage of the kitchen boy. We all know how after Spitzer's defeat peace reigned for such a short time, and how evil poured through the Guardian Mountain. Evil, led by King Orcam of Sodah. We know of the challenge made upon the King by that young kitchen boy, now an eighteen year old captain in the army of Arac. We know how Orcam was defeated in single combat and returned through the secret way to Sodah. how that small kitchen boy, who became a young captain, eventually became the great and good King Synod. All of these things, we know. We also know how Orcam swore that one day his sons or the sons of his sons would return to Arac and put her in chains. How the secret way was lost to Sodah but found by Synod during his twelve year vigil in the mountains that now bear his name. We know these things, some as history, some as legend.

We also know the Prophecy of the True Word, but, what do we know?"

The King now stopped and was silent for some minutes. He looked around the Great Hall and saw one of his own kitchen boys standing beside the King's steward. He called to the boy. "Boy, I know you from our kitchens but do not recall your name."

The boy was red with the embarrassment of being singled out in such a gathering.

"My name is Donys Sire," the boy stuttered.

"Come to me Donys," the King smiled and beckoned.

Prompted by the King's steward, a big, bluff but friendly man, the boy bowed and approached the King. He stopped at the bottom of the three steps that led to the King's throne.

"Don't be afraid," said the King, "come and stand by me." He walked slowly up the steps and stood facing, a little to the right of the King.

"Now Donys, do you know the history of Arac?"

"Yes Sire," answered the boy.

"And do you understand the legend of The Secret Way?"

"I think so Sire, the way was discovered by King Orcam of Sodah.

There is no other way over or through the Mountains of Synod. After Orcam died the secret died with him, and it was known to no man, until, near the end of his life our Great King Synod rediscovered the way."

"And do you understand the 'Prophecy of the True Word?'" said the King." The boy nodded.

THE DREAM

"Then tell us all the story Donys, as you learned it."

The boy took a deep breath and launched into the Prophecy that every child was taught almost before they learned to speak.

"Beyond the mountains in the north
There lies a land, both cruel and coarse.
They call it Sodah and 'tis well
To know that evil there does dwell.
Through some freak chance when time was young
When men still spoke a common tongue,
The mountains gave a secret track
That led from Sodah to Arac.
A man more wicked than the rest
Put this track to fearful test.
His name was mighty – as his sword,
'Tis he who led his fearsome hoard
From Sodah's rough and barren sands
to Arac's green and pleasant lands –
His aim to capture, then to reign
And crush those who spoke freedoms name.
But fate was kind, a challenge and
This warrior died – by Synods hand
The Secret Way died with his death
And, cursing, he, with dying breath,
Proclaimed that Arac fear the day
That one like he would tread the way,
The Secret Way, that he had found
And raze the country to the ground.
Arac would know peace – never more,
Arac must always hone for war.

THE THIRTEENTH KNIGHT

The passing of a thousand years
Will not reduce her crippling fears
To live whole lives, this burden borne
At any time their land be torn
Apart – and they to stand condemned.
Their land they failed to defend.
But Synod found the Secret Way,
But cannot tell until the day
That all the signs are pointing high;
When brave young men prepare to die
Will close for ere the secret path,
While through it Sodah's hoards still pass
Then Sodah's might will fail its test,
And only then Arac will rest."

"Well-done Donys" said King Pylon, "you have learned the legend well. Do you also know the Prophecy?" The boy nodded,

"The Prophecy of the True Word says that one day the warlike hoards from Sodah, that barren and inhospitable land beyond the mountains ..." Donys repeated the words that he and all Aracians were taught as children. "Will once more discover the secret way lost at the time of Orcam, and will surge through the mountains like an unstoppable river to put Arac and its people in chains for ever." He stopped and took another deep breath. "But during the Vigil of Synod and with the help of the Keeper of the Gate, twelve Tokens were fashioned, and twelve words delivered.

These were entrusted to the twelve bravest

young men in the kingdom, to be handed down from son to son until the Prophecy be fulfilled."

"And HOW will the Prophecy be fulfilled?" asked the King.

"When the Tokens were joined, and the True Word spoken," said the boy, "a stranger will come who will seal the secret way forever."

"Do we know who this stranger is, or from whence he will come?" said the King.

"We know only," answered Donys, "that he will be not of our world."

The King placed his arm around the boy's shoulders. "My subjects," he said, "Donys is right. He has recited the Prophecy as we know it, as we have been taught it. But there is more, it has always been the burden of the King to carry a knowledge that sits in the mind whether waking or sleeping. The knowledge is not of how the prophecy will be fulfilled. Nor is it whether we will know victory and peace, or defeat and bondage; but of the Seven Parts through which the prophecy must pass if it is to be fulfilled."

He stood up, tall and regal. "The time has come for me to share the knowledge that my Knights and I have, until now, held alone."

King Pylon then told them of his Knights, of their Visions, of Prince Gemree, of his Dream, of Pimm, of The Journey to come, of the Ordeals of the Sacrifice, of the Follower and of the Thirteenth Knight. The people were spellbound as the King's voice rang out, filling the furthurmost corners of the Great Hall.

"And so," the King concluded two of the Seven Parts – The Visions and The Dream are completed and the Third, The Journey has been revealed to me. One amongst us has been designated to make that journey, and I must seek him out by the asking of a riddle." The King, who had been walking around the Great Hall as he spoke, now returned to his throne and sat down.

The waters deep, the waters blue flow over me, flow over you,
We know not where the waters go
But will return from whence they flow."

The King stood up again and pointed at his subjects. "The Prophecy says that there is one amongst you who can answer that riddle. It is upon him that the burden, and indeed the honour of undertaking the most important journey in Arac's history will fall. Please retire now, all of you, and on the stroke of midnight let those who believe that they can answer the riddle which The Prophecy has set, come to me."

The people quietly filed from the Great Hall until only the King and his eleven Knights were left. They did not speak but sat quietly as the flame of the clock candles slowly marked the passing hours.

Clannnng!!! The deep chime of the bell in the hand of the Time Steward signified the first stroke of midnight as the flame licked over the candles' marking. Clannnng!!! Clannnng!!! Clannnng!!!. The huge oak door to the Great Hall remained firmly closed. Clannnng!!! Clannnng!!!.

THE DREAM

"The Prophecy demands" said the King speaking softly and almost to himself, "that the riddle must be answered on the last stroke of midnight. Not a moment before or a moment after, only then can the Prophecy be fulfilled." Clannnng!!! Clannnng!!!

"Eight" said a voice, it was Prince Edmund. He sat nervously on the edge of his ornate, high-backed chair.

Clannnng!!! Clannnng!!!

"Ten," said the King.

Clannnng!!! Cla – "Please Sire, it is The Saddlestone" – nnng!!!.

The King started, the voice had come not from the Great Oak Door at the far end of the Great Hall, but from the curtained alcove that led to the Robing Room, behind the Kings Throne. The King turned round, but the heavy drapes still hung over the opening and there was no-one to be seen.

"Whose voice is that?" said the King.

"Please Sire, I'm sorry, it is I, Pimm, squire to Prince Gemree," the small voice spoke quietly. "A force that I cannot explain directed me to this place at this time. A voice, which did not feel like my own, called out as the last bell chimed. But Sire, I know that riddle, and I know that the answer is correct"

"Come, show yourself Pimm," said the King. The small figure of the squire with his red tights, and his silver buckled shoes, walked quietly to his place, beside the chair of the twelfth Knight.

"The Prophecy was right," said the King, though not in the way I expected. But even now, it is required that you give not only the answer to the riddle, but your reasons for that answer."

"Sire," began Pimm, "where the River Titch meets the Forest of Hanlon and the Plains of Oblivia, there is a ford. When the waters are low there are rocks that rise high above the water's surface like steps. In the centre of the ford is a rock larger than the rest and shaped like a huge saddle, so much so that men call this 'The Saddlestone'. When the waters run high, which is often, all but the Saddlestone are hidden beneath the surface, and men rest in their crossing upon the island rock." Pimm paused but was motioned to continue by the King. "There is a legend that says that The Saddlestone once sat at the very source of the River Titch. That during the great floods at the time of the Oblivian it was washed hundreds of miles down the river to its present home. It is said that one day The Saddlestone will return to the river's source, and that that will herald the start of the Prophecy's fulfilment"

"And why do you believe that 'The Saddlestone' is the answer to the riddle?" said the King.

Pimm did not answer immediately, and then said. "Your Majesty, on our journey to the Mountains of Synod, my master and I have to cross the river. Always we cross at the ford of The Saddlestone. On our last journey, when we arrived at the bank of the river, we came across a very old man. He was small and frail. The river was a raging torrent following the mountain's storms and all the rocks were hidden, save The Saddlestone. It was clear to my master that the old man could not cross. He bent down and took him into his arms. The old man started singing softly as Prince Gemree fought the violent waters that tried to pluck him off his feet. When they reached The Saddlestone they rested, and leaving the old man safely above the water my master returned to help me across. When we reached The Saddlestone the old man had gone, yet somehow we were not dismayed. Some inner knowledge told us that the old man was safe. Strangely enough, although the saddlestone was empty his song still hung in the air.

My master and I accepted the happening as a part of our strange journey and I thought no more until this evening when I heard you say those words. I know now that the words the old man was singing, the words left hanging over the empty Saddlestone were -

The waters deep, the waters blue,
flow over me, flow over you,
We know not where the waters go.
But will return from whence they flow."

Pimm looked into the King's eyes. "I now know, Sire, that the old man was a part of the Prophecy, as surely as I know that The Saddlestone is the answer to your riddle and will play an important part in its fulfilment."

THE THIRTEENTH KNIGHT

The King smiled down at the tiny figure of Pimm, the squire.

"Pimm," he said quietly, "you are the one who has been chosen.

You are the one who must follow Prince Gemree along the path that he has cleared. You are the one who must return with the Stranger who holds the key to the salvation of Arac. You must seek and find The Thirteenth Knight. You, are The Follower.

Go now, and Good Speed."

Chapter Seven

The Journey Starts

Lands of the east awake
Now may your sons break free
The sleep of the ages break
Rise now, to victory …

For as far as the eye could see, from the forests in the west, to the mighty sea in the east, the armies stood. Men and horses, cannon and lance. They covered the plains like ants upon a honey jar. Still, unmoving, silent.

And then the trumpets began. First one, then another, until ten thousand trumpets called one million men to arms. The mass shuddered and then began to move, line formed upon line, column formed upon column. The slow relentless march towards the Guardian Mountains and the Secret Way had started.

Pimm could hear the children laughing. He had a vague idea that they were laughing at him, but suddenly the children were no longer important. Far in the distance he could hear Miss Colbran saying "Sit down now Francis" but Miss Colbran was no longer important either. All that mattered was that at last he remembered. Triggered by the circle of chairs he knew who he was, where he was, where he came from and *most* important – *why he was here.*

It had been dark when Pimm had left the palace of King Pylon. He had stopped only long enough to collect some food from the castle kitchens. Donys the kitchen boy, who now felt very important, had helped him. Donys had begged to be allowed to go along with Pimm, but Pimm knew that The Prophecy demanded that he make the journey alone.

King Pylon had even ventured down into the kitchens to talk to him while the food was being prepared. He had taken him to one side and spoken earnestly for some minutes.

"Pimm," he had said, "the way before you is long and dangerous. Prince Gemree has gone before you to clear your path. You have been chosen for a mighty task it is a task at which, for the sake of Arac, you must not fail. I am sure that you are equal to the demands that will be made upon you. Remember always that you will be following the footsteps of your master. If you falter in courage or resolve, then his brave sacrifice will have been in vain. We *will* meet again only if your courage is equal to Gemree's sacrifice and his sacrifice is equal to your courage. I pray, my Knights pray, the people pray that we will meet again – for then Arac will have been saved." The King felt a tugging at the hem of his cloak, he looked down, there looking up at him was Donys.

"Sire," the small boy said, "please may I travel with Pimm to help him? I can make a fire, I can carry his pack, I could cook his food, I …"?

"Stop," the King interrupted with a laugh, "and be still, Pimm is making a journey that can only be made alone. BUT …" he said, seeing the disappointment creep across the boys face, "he has a journey of many days before his real journey can start. I am sure that he will be very glad of your company until then." The boy clapped his hands, and turning again to Pimm, the King said "Donys will be good company for you in that part of your journey when you need not be alone with your thoughts. Let him accompany you to The Saddlestone. You can leave him there, I will see that he is kept safe." The King placed his hands on Pimm's shoulders, and then turned and walked swiftly up the stone staircase, without a backward glance. Pimm waited but a moment or two, and then, with a cheerful "Come on then young Donys, we have far to go" he began his journey of destiny.

The journey to the ford where The Saddlestone lay was a familiar one for Pimm, but still arduous and boring. Many times he blessed the King's wisdom for letting the boy come along. The little fellow was a constant joy – and through his reaction to the many new experiences, Pimm himself found a new delight in the things that surrounded them. "Pimm, what is that blue flower called? Pimm, why can that bird soar so high?

Pimm, have you ever travelled through that great forest?" Pimm spent so much of his time answering young Donys' questions that he had little time to dwell upon what lay ahead. It was just as the King had predicted.

Each night when they stopped, Donys scurried around collecting wood and brush to make a fire which he then cleverly lit without any fuss at all. He arranged a 'spit' from which to hang and cook the salted meat and other foods he had packed. He laid out Pimm's bedroll and made the most delicious hot drink from berries that he found and water from the many streams that crossed their paths. Pimm knew that it was going to be very hard to say goodbye to the young boy when they reached The Saddlestone. He also knew that he had made a friend for ever.

Day passed day, and night passed night without incident. As evening approached on the tenth day they saw the great junction where the plain, the forest and the river met, ahead of them. Pimm, camped some distance from the ford, as not knowing what he would find at his Journey's start, he preferred to arrive there alone, and in the daylight. Donys, sensing that their parting was close was even more attentive that night. When they had eaten their food, and drunk their hot berry drink, when he had laid out their bedrolls, and piled the fire high to last through till the dawn, he looked at Pimm. For the first time since they set out, his face was sad, and his voice tearful.

"I know you must leave me tomorrow, and I know the journey you are going on is very dangerous and that you may not come back." He looked wistful. "Pimm" he said, "what do you know of your journey?"

Pimm shook his head slowly. "I know nothing " he said, "I trust the Prophecy to guide my steps."

"Pimm," said Donys "I understand nought of what I now speak, even the language seems old and strange. My being here is not an accident — although I have enjoyed the journey greatly," he added quickly. "Because of what has happened to me, I believe that King Pylon picked me out for a reason. You remember how, in the Great Hall, I was asked to tell what I knew of the Prophecy."

"I do," said Pimm " and you spoke well"

"That night," continued Donys, "after I had returned to my attic room, I had a visitor. I know that it was the old King Synod. He told me that I had an important part to play in the Prophecy, and that I would be the one to help you at the start of your journey. The King said that it was fitting that a lowly kitchen boy, just as he himself had been, should be chosen. He said that my part in the Prophecy was pre-destined."

"What happened next?" said Pimm.

The King told me that I was to go to the Kitchens and prepare food for the journey, that I was to ask you to let me accompany you on your journey. He said that you would resist but that I would get an unexpected ally — that of course was King Pylon. I asked him how I was to help you. He told me not to worry, but that when the time was right I would know exactly what I must do and say." The boy turned and faced The Saddlestone ford in the distance. "The time has arrived" he said, "and there is a jumble of words in my head. Let us sit Pimm, and I will tell you what I know."

The two sat down facing each other. Pimm drew his little legs up to his chin and, wrapping his arms around his knees, rocked slowly backwards and forwards. Donys closed his eyes and sat with his legs crossed and his back straight. He was quiet for some moments, and then he began to speak in a soft but resonant voice that seemed not to be his, but to be the voice of an older, wiser man.

"Twelve times the Secret Way is broken
To mark each place I give a Token
This Token gives both clue and key,
When locked together you will see
Power of wind and sun and rain
Will close the Secret Way again
But twelve brave Knights may die before
The way is closed forever more.
That's why I called before my throne
Twelve young men, who each alone
Will hold a Token and pass on
His burden to his youngest son,
Who one day in a future age
Will share a vision with one Page.
Twelve Knights and one brave squire will lead

THE JOURNEY STARTS

A Thirteenth Knight who will succeed
In crushing Sodah for all time,
But 'Courage Mountain' first to climb.
Who is this Page, the one to play
That vital part upon the day?
A squire whose name will always live
Whenever men of Arac give
Their homage to the Knights so brave
They'll add the name of Pimm – a Page.
Who, unasked, fulfilled his destiny
by following his Lord – Gemree.
Like restless seas follow the tide,
Through gateways Gemree's opened wide,
Pimm must go to a world unknown
To seek a stranger – all alone,
And bring him back to stand and face
Our Lord Gemree's most special place,
The Tablestone, at river's source,
The Tokens are in place – of course
The Knights will reach out with their hands
And close the way that links our lands,
But if the Stranger does not come
before the Tokens' work is done
Then all the power will be cocooned
And Arac be forever doomed.
And now the journey you must start,
Be strong of will and brave of heart
Remember well these words I say,
The old man will point you to the way."

Donys opened his eyes. He looked blankly at
Pimm and had no recollection of the words that

had been spoken through him.

"Have I helped you Pimm?" he said

Pimm smiled, "Yes, Donys, you have helped beyond measure, sleep now, for tomorrow we must part."

The sun had barely started its ascent into the eastern sky when Pimm arrived at The Saddlestone. The day was calm, and the sky had changed from that deep purple of early dawn, to a deep restful blue. The trees were still, there was not a breath of wind to stir the air. The waters of the ford were low and calm, with the Saddlestone thrust high above the surface, and the stepping stones within easy reach. Pimm knew that his journey must start from the Saddlestone. He began to make his way to the river bank to take the small step to the first of the raised stones.

"Greetings young sir," said a quavering old voice, "I knew that you would return, though now I observe, more purpose points your way."

"Old man," said Pimm, "Now I understand that which was hidden from me before – you are part of the Prophecy."

"The waters deep. The waters blue" chuckled the old man.

"How can I serve you best?" said Pimm.

"My dear young sir," said the old man, "you serve me not at all, I am here to serve you. But first, please carry me to The Saddlestone, the river runs high today and the stepping stones hide from our sight."

Pimm started to protest that the old man was

quite wrong, but as he turned towards the river he saw it was in full flood. Where, just moments ago the stepping stones had risen high above the water, now they were not to be seen; although the white tops of the tumbling waters showed where the stones lay inches below the surface.

"Old man" said Pimm "When last we were at this place, I watched my Master, Prince Gemree, lift you and carry you across these turbulent waters. My master is tall and strong, his legs are long and powerful. Yet he struggled through waters that reached above his waist and buffeted and tugged so that I felt he must surely fall. I am small and have not one tenth the strength of my master, yet you will trust my arms to carry you through the torrent?"

The old man smiled, "I have waited through many centuries for the Prophecy to be fulfilled – have faith in me Pimm, as I have faith in you. You have much to learn and understand, but you have much more to take on trust. Come, lift me and we will rest upon The Saddlestone whilst I point you forward on your Journey."

Pimm lifted the old man into his short stubby arms and it was as if he lifted a feather. He stepped into the water which, should have come high upon his body – yet his feet seemed not to reach the rocky bed of the river, and though his steps were firm the raging torrent plucked but gently at his ankles. He waded forward with confident stride and was soon placing his burden gently upon The Saddlestone.

When they were both safely on The Saddlestone watching the waters seethe and bubble below them, Pimm spoke.

"Tell me old man," he said, "I understand that I have a destiny to fulfil, I understand its importance, and although I do not understand why I have been chosen, I will willingly do as I am bidden." He stopped and looked at the old man who was smiling softly. "But," Pimm went on "how can I fulfil anything when I am told I must go to an unknown world and find a stranger who will become the Thirteenth Knight of Arac? I don't know where I must go, I don't know how I will get there, I don't know how I will recognise this stranger. Even if I do all of those things, I have absolutely no idea how to get him back to the Tablestone at the source of the River Titch." Pimm felt quite out of breath after this long speech, and looked imploringly at the old man. For once the old man stopped smiling. He placed his hands on Pimm's shoulders and looked at him earnestly.

"You must not worry about any of these things. Your destiny is mapped out for you and each step of your way will be revealed only after the step before has been completed. Now, all that is required of you is that you sleep and rest.

Your journey will begin soon and before you goes your master, the Prince Gemree to clear your way. "

Pimm closed his eyes. He could hear the waters swirling just below The Saddlestone. He could hear the wind whistling as it whipped the small crests of the wavelets and tore them from the surface of the water, flinging them high in the air. He heard these things – and yet – the air around him felt calm. He closed his eyes, and then he slept.

Chapter Eight

The Ordeals

Prince Gemree knew that Pimm would be watching him until he finally vanished from his sight, but he did not look back. He knew that he would need all his resolve and all his courage if he were to succeed in the journey and the Ordeals that lay before him. The dream had revealed a great deal to him, and yet, it had revealed nothing at all. He could not reconcile the dream's unreality with the reality that surrounded him, as he pointed the head of his horse high up towards the mountains of Synod.

He allowed the dream to play once more through his mind. His journey had started at the source of the Titch where he had plunged through the deep waters, that were not water at all – but beautiful waterfalls filled with rainbow colours. He recalled his nightmare descent through purple blackness. A blackness relieved only by the fiery brightness of the evil eyes of huge bats. Their wings unfurled like flags and then wrapped around their dry, rustling bodies like cloaks. After the cavern of the bats he remembered the dream controlled terror of the bottomless pit. Sides, sheer and shiny rose a hundred feet into the inky nothingness above, upon whose slime covered floor writhed and slithered, raced and scuttled a horrifying jumble of snakes and lizards. The sounds had intensified the horror of a sight denied to the eyes in the ebony darkness. Gemree let his mind dwell lingeringly upon the peace and tranquillity of the scene that had then followed. Of the fields of corn, of the lush green forests, of the placid blue lakes, and gently flowing rivers. He recalled the beautiful maiden and allowed her face and form to linger in his mind. Then he forced it onwards, to the demonic castle defended by the evil Knight of Rantoc. Then again, that vision of pure love-liness, the maiden. And finally, the Great Iron Gates with their malevolent and demanding Keeper. He shuddered involuntarily as he thought of the Keeper's demand. The price for the key that opened the gates to the other world. His willing and unresisting sacrifice, which would allow the Follower to find the stranger who was to be the Thirteenth Knight and the saviour of Arac.

Gemree counted the Ordeals through his mind. The Waterfalls, The Cavern of Bats, The Pit of Snakes, The Beautiful Maiden, The Knight of Rantoc, The Gates of The Trueworld, and the Final Sacrifice.

Gradually his journey took shape in his mind. He knew that he must pass through each of the seven stages of his journey to make it safe for the Follower. That at none of the stages must he fail.

Nothing must stop him opening the Great Gates at journey's end. He prayed that his courage would not let him down. He dug his heels into the flanks of his mighty steed and turned his head high into the Mountains of Synod and the source of the Titch.

Gemree dismounted, it had taken many days to follow the river from The Saddlestone, northwards and ever higher into the mountains. Now it lay before him: a deep, though disappointingly small pool lying in a basin formed by a ring of huge boulders. Gemree remembered how, in his dream, it had seemed that the mountain peaks themselves had moulded themselves into the basin's sides, and that a great lake had been formed thereby. He searched his mind in case a forgotten portion of his dream might hold the key to the next step of his journey. He remembered how he had seemed to plunge into the lake from a great height. How he had first tumbled, then floated through the water that somehow, was not water. He was bewildered, he sat on the bank throwing stone after stone into the depths and watching the ripples gradually widen and then disappear.

All through a crisp calm day, and a cold but still night Gemree sat and wondered. With the dawn of the next day, black clouds rolled down from the mountain tops. Slowly at first, but then with ever increasing intensity rain drops started to fall. Soon rain was sheeting across the face of the landscape and hitting the surface of the pool with great force. Rain drops bounced high into the air, as if to return to the clouds that had ejected them. Huge puddles formed on the ground around the lake; soon the puddles had joined together to make riverlets that poured off the banks into the pool. Gemree had to seek higher ground and leading his horse he forced a way higher and higher up the mountain slopes. Soon he was level with the very tops of the boulders that formed the steep walls of the pool. He made no attempt to shelter but, withdrawn into his thoughts he stared almost unseeingly into the waters below. As he stared, he became aware of two facts that took on great importance. Although the pool was small in area, and water was now gushing into it from all sides in great torrents, the level remained unmoved. Gemree took a mark, clearly to be seen on the opposite wall. Always the water lapped gently against this line, never rising above it.

From his position perched high above the pool, he realised that the scene below him was just as it had been in his dream, as he floated down from a great height towards the surface of the lake. For a long time he looked hard at the surface of the pool, examining each corner minutely. After a while he noticed that there was an area of turbulence where the two huge boulders on the opposite side of the pool met. He stared fixedly at this point for many minutes, and noticed that the water's level in the pool did not rise. As fast as the water flooded in, so it rushed out. Fleetingly he allowed himself to ponder. If the water gushes out at such a speed, why does the pool not empty when the rains are not replenishing it? And then, if the water flows out at such a rate, where is it going? There are no cliffs, there are no ravines or gorges. The waters can only be surging deeper and deeper underground.

In a final moment Gemree made his decision. Courage, he had been told was the devotion he needed most in facing his ordeal. What greater courage could there be than to leap into the unknown? He stood up and turning to his horse he untethered his reins and slapped his rump.

"Go good friend," he said, "make your way down the mountainside to safety. You have served me well and I will miss you greatly, but what I have now to do I must do alone." Turning, Gemree launched himself head first into the bubbling waters below.

The icy coldness bit into his very heart as he hit the surface. Gemree knew as he dived that, if his hope was unfounded, his silver armour would make any chance of his reaching the surface again impossible. He had aimed himself at the point where the two boulders met and as he went deeper and deeper he could feel the strength of the water adding speed to his own momentum as the current plucked at him and dragged him to the opening from where, as he had guessed, the water cascaded through the very bed of the pool. His lungs were bursting; great pains pounded in his chest. Just as he thought he must surely fail in his mission at the very first step, the pressure of the water increased beyond all reckoning. Gemree found himself ejected with great force, through a hole barely larger than himself, into bright and glorious sunshine. He was falling, he was falling through water – and yet he could breath as water touched upon him and then turned to the side. He was falling through the largest, most beautiful rainbow – no, a hundred, a thousand of the most beautiful rainbows he had ever seen.

Why he could not say but although he was now falling faster and faster, somehow he knew that he would be safe.

What he was looking at was an exact reproduction of the dream that had seemed so impossible. He turned and tumbled lazily as he fell; now in, now out of the cascading water. No longer icy cold, but now with the warmth of a soothing balm. And then with no warning he stopped his descent as if caught in the arms of a passing giant. So immediate was the arresting of his downward plunge that all the breath was forced out of his body and for some minutes he lost all consciousness. When he came to, he found that his face was pressed tightly against a sweet smelling softness the like of which he had never known. He was lying face down, and carefully, not knowing where he was, he began to edge himself onto his side, and then very slowly onto his back and finally into a sitting position. The sight that was now before him was the most wonderful he had ever seen, and yet he knew it must surely be a world of pure fantasy.

High above him, many hundreds of feet above him, great craggy cliffs soared into a sky that was as blue as the shield that bore his Sacred Sign of Arac. The face of this majestic rock face was regularly punctuated by openings from which water tumbled and rushed, surged and plummeted: a jumble of colour and shape. Water from one opening mingled and mashed with water from other openings. There stood against the backdrop of the rocky cliffs a tapestry of shape and colour such as there had surely never been before. And yet, even that was not all.

In this deep blue sky a bright yellow sun sent its rays into the tumbling waters. Each droplet, with facets like diamonds, reflected colours of different intensity and hue.

One thousand rainbows danced in one thousand airborne rivers, as the waters of one world emptied themselves into the eager grasp of another. Gemree realised that he had been projected through one of these many openings hundreds of feet above his head. He wondered, how could a mere mortal survive such a fall, as he appeared to have done.

He now began to look more carefully at where he lay. He looked right and left. Close to his left side a deep but narrow river caught the waterfalls. To the right, and for as far as the eye could see, lay a lush deep green surface. This formed a thick green cushion upon which he seemed to have landed. All around him the cascading waters fell, but as they landed, they seemed to disappear leaving the green surface with a wet sheen, but no more. Gemree dug his hand down into the soft, unresisting greenness. Down and down it went. The surface seemed to have the consistency of loosely woven moss, the roots forming themselves into a cat's cradle of strands – almost like a huge net. The green foliage filled the holes between, like down in a mattress. Amongst the greenness were occasional patches of bright coloured flowers, reds and blues, silvers and golds. In the sky birds sang, and butterflies flitted from bloom to bloom. Briefly Gemree thought: could this be paradise? His mind's eye saw his body still lying at the bottom of an icy cold mountain pool, weighed down by its armour. But then he thought of his dream and realised how his experience, however long it had lasted, a minute, an hour, or a day, was exactly as the dream sent to him by Synod had depicted. No, he smiled happily, this was not paradise, this was no dream. He had completed the first Ordeal with courage and success. His was not the duty to wonder how, to wonder if, to wonder why. His duty was clear, to face the Ordeals, to clear the way for The Follower, and finally to sacrifice himself to the keeper of the Great Gates of the Trueworld. Gemree stood up, and with bouncy step started walking towards the sun, now slowly setting beyond the horizon.

Chapter Nine

The Follower

When Pimm awoke the old man had gone. The waters were calm and once again both The Saddlestone and the stepping stones were clearly visible above the surface.

"Well, what do I do now?" Pimm said out loud, but to himself for all that.

"There is nothing for you to do, but put your faith in Prince Gemree and the Prophecy." Pimm heard the voice speaking even though there was no-one to be seen.

"When the storm is over many things will have become clearer to you, and you will soon be on The Saddlestone at the source of the River Titch."

Pimm turned in a full circle seeking out the source of the voice but, except for Donys, he was alone. He looked at the boy, but he still lay in a deep sleep. Not for one moment did it occur to Pimm that the boy should not be there, nor did he wonder how he had crossed the swollen river alone. Feeling rather foolish Pimm said – "But the day is fine, there is no storm. Look at the stillness of the trees, look how the water ripples gently against The Saddlestone – which rests here, NOT at the river's source." The voice was markedly softer as it said. "Look to the mountains; it is from there that the storm will come, rising at the very source of the river. It is to that source that both you and The Saddlestone will be carried to begin your journey."

Pimm looked up into the clear blue sky and, almost without warning it began to darken. He turned and faced the mountains and was startled to see great rolling cloudS tumbling down the long distant slopes. Then they were sweeping over the flat plains. Their edges touched the outer ranks of trees in the Boldeg Forests and almost bent them double with their strength and their fury. Although the storm was still many miles away, Pimm could hear the loud cracks of thunder and could see the lightning as huge forks lit up the undersides of the angry black clouds. Donys awoke suddenly and was frightened. Pimm had time only to say "Fear not Donys, we are safe; what we see now and will experience shortly, is no more than has been foretold by the Prophecy." Donys grasped his arm and his eyes widened with fear as the water, which moments before had been gently rippling against The Saddlestone, now began to bubble and seethe. Within moments the stepping stones were no longer visible and The Saddlestone remained only inches above the chattering crests of the white and turbulent foam. The rain started slowly, and then began to beat on their unprotected bodies faster and faster until Pimm felt that the very force of the rain drops would wash them both from their perch. And then the wind started. Never had there been such fury. It plucked at their clothes, it forced the breath out of their bodies. Only by lying flat, face down upon The Saddlestone and hanging grimly on to each other and to any small crevices that they could find did they prevent themselves from being flung bodily into the now raging torrent which surrounded them. For what seemed a lifetime, lightning flashed around them. The wind was relentless in its banshee howls, and the rain beat upon them in curtains of chain link. All around them the river raged, frequently sending exploratory fingers across The Saddlestone as if unhappy at the failure of the wind and rain, and the thunder and the lightning to dislodge them from the precarious safety of The Saddlestone. Pimm and Donys lay sobbing in discomfort and fear.

And then it was over. In seconds the wind slowed to a whisper, the thunder stopped and there was a feeling of great peace. The rain still beat upon them relentlessly, and the lightning continued to flash. But now there was a different quality about it as if all its anger had gone. Pimm could no longer hear the wrath and fury of the water slapping against the sides of The Saddlestone. He felt The Saddlestone, its surface was spongy and unresisting to his probing touch. He stood up and immediately sank down into the soft, green, mossy, sweet smelling ground. He looked down, he could not see his legs from the knees downwards and yet, although they had sunk into this strange surface they were not gripped. He lifted his leg and his foot came clear of the ground easily only to vanish again as he put his weight back on to it.

He looked up and realised that there was no rain. There was no lightning. He was standing beneath a million waterfalls. Rainbows of the most delicious colours played in the cascading water. What he thought had been lightning flashes were no more than the warm and beautiful sunlight bouncing its colours off the many faceted droplets of water. Of The Saddlestone there was no sign. Beside him Donys had also been taking in the wonders that now lay before them.

"Pimm," he said, "where is this wonderful place?"

"I don't know," said Pimm with a shrug, "but Donys, I do believe that our journey has begun."

Prince Gemree had no sooner stood up and taken his first step forward across the strange spongy landscape than he found himself waist deep in the sweet smelling, lightly clinging plants. He removed his leg easily but, once more sank deeply as he moved forward. It was like walking in deep snow, and within a few dozen steps, fit and strong as he was, he was beginning to feel a dull ache in his muscles. Shielding his eyes he stared into the distance, and realised that he would never cover that vast landscape unless he could devise a way to make his progress easier. No sooner had that thought entered his head, than another followed, although this felt more like a voice from outside than a thought conjured from within his own mind.

"Remember your purpose as demanded by the Prophecy. Yours is not simply to complete a journey and to overcome great dangers. You must clear the way for The Follower. You must ensure that no danger or entrapments await him." The voice was gone almost before the sound faded from his brain.

"Of course" Gemree punched a clenched fist against the palm of his hand. "I must clear and mark the way, otherwise my journey is for nothing." He sank down upon the yielding surface, closed his eyes, and settled into deep thought.

"The problem," Gemree said softly to himself, "is a simple one: I must think, not of the whole journey, but of its parts. If I solve all the parts, then I also solve the whole." In his mind he stood, and took a tentative step forward. He saw his foot, then his leg disappear beneath the surface. Down, and down, it went as the small area of ground upon which he placed his weight failed to support him.

He lay flat upon the surface with his arms and legs outstretched like a star. The plant gave a little, no more than a slight indentation as his weight was spread over a wide area of the surface. Now it was obvious that he could not walk over the strange landscape because he would keep sinking deeply below its surface. Equally, it was obvious that he could not continue to lie spreadeagled. His progress would be so slow that he would surely die of hunger before he had covered a fraction of the distance. He continued to meditate. There appeared to be no danger, or risk to his life whilst on this huge plant. He began to look about him; until now he had looked only away from the cliffs out of which the water poured. He had only looked in the direction that he believed his path could lie. He now swivelled his body and looked towards the towering rock face of the waterfall.

He was on the edge of the green area of land only a few feet away from a swiftly flowing river. In places, small clumps of this plant broke away from the main mass and went spinning on their unknown journey, following the tumbling currents. Prince Gemree smiled, for here lay his answer. He drew his sword, and experimentally thrust it down into the unresisting moss. After a few moments he had detached an area about the size of a small table. He held onto it for a moment or two and then let it go, watching it go dancing away. Again he thrust his sword downwards, this time painstakingly shredding the foliage from the roots until he drew forth a white and wiry stem ten feet or so in length. He now knew that his plan would work. For many hours Gemree worked with sword and hands. Eventually, there bobbed up and down on the water two of the strangest little craft you have ever seen. Each was about ten feet long and three feet wide. Each was, of course, deep green in colour. There was a deep recess in the centre where a full-grown man could lie and have the high sides protect him from the elements. At the front of the boat there was a sturdy rope formed by plaiting together many strands of the plant's own roots, ones which formed the land, and which Gemree had already named 'Plantmass.' Each craft was tugged by the current, but held fast by its anchoring rope. The rear of the boat, which was rounded, had fixed over it a large, broad, flat mat – solid where it had been woven over and over itself. From its flatness protruded a thick plaited tiller to give the movement to steer this sturdy little vessel. Gemree rested, well pleased with his labours, which had provided the means to leave this clinging land mass and proceeding on his journey into the unknown.

Gemree had no doubts that The Follower would be guided to where the boat lay; but, to ensure that his work was not in vain, he had carefully cut away at the green leaves of the plant on the bow of the boat. Where the daylight shone through, the name "The Lord Gemree" was clearly visible. Happy that he had accomplished this part of his task, Gemree stepped into the forward boat. With a single blow of his sword he cut the rope just where it joined the Plantmass, and in a moment was spinning away, down the river and out of sight.

Chapter Ten

The Cavern

The little boat had lain straining as the plaited roots held her against the river's eager current. The speed with which she had rocketed away from the Plantmass, as Gemree sliced the anchoring rope with his sword, took his breath away, and left him a jumble of arms and legs on the boat's spongy deck. He clambered back on to his feet, laughing and exhilarated as the small craft danced and darted in and out of the flying spray.

Never had a boat been so seaworthy, so unsinkable. Such water as splashed into her small, sword fashioned cockpit, simply drained through and back into the river. Unlike a conventional craft, were they to be swept into a rock or other hazard the hull would simply dent, and then spring back into place. Like a floating leaf or branch, there was no force that could take and keep that natural buoyancy below the water's surface.

Gemree had, of course, realised that if he tried to stand up in the boat his feet would sink through the bottom, just as they had sunk into the plant mass from where his journey had started. He had therefore made further and clever use of the strong root formations from which he had fashioned the ropes and the rudder. He had woven a firm mat of roots which lay the full length and width of both boats. This formed a floor which was not only solid and comfortable to walk on, but also still allowed the water to drain through it. With a light and excited heart, Gemree stood up in the bow of the little vessel and let his destiny and the Prophecy take its course.

The river ran swiftly between the huge towering cliffs to his left, and the long unbroken expanse of green plant mass to his right. In places the river narrowed to no more than a small country lane, at others it was wider even than the Great River Titch in his beloved Arac. From time to time the boat was swept into the rocky cliff face, but always it simply bounced off into the middle of the river again. Provided Gemree kept his arms safely inside the boat so that they could not get crushed, he was in no danger. Now and again the boat would be washed to the other side of the river and bang against the spongy green Plantmass, but here again no danger threatened. The river seemed to stretch for ever. Gemree, his hand shielding his eyes from the ever bright sunlight, stared forward. He knew that he must prepare himself for a long journey. For the first time since his arrival in this strange world, he began to think about food, or rather the empty feeling in his stomach prodded his brain into the thought.

THE CAVERN

He had discovered whilst he was building the boats, that the river water was clear, fresh, and sweet tasting, so thirst was going to be no problem.

The Plantmass seemed to support no life whatsoever, so clearly there was no source of sustenance to be had from that direction. High above the river huge gulls and other birds dived and soared, but they never came down towards the river's surface. From this observation alone, Gemree realised that the river obviously supported no fish, so he could not look in that direction for sustenance. He sat in the stern of the boat. Although steering the craft was not a priority, he tucked the tiller under his arm and made a course as close to the centre of the river as possible. Then he focused his mind upon the problem of his ever increasing hunger. As he sat, he carelessly picked up a stray piece of the root matting on the floor of the boat. Casually, he stuck it between his teeth in much the same way as a farm labourer would suck on a piece of straw. But here, all similarity ended. The root was sweet tasting and with the consistency of a vegetable such as a turnip, although more flexible. He quickly chewed his way through this small piece of root and found that in addition to its very acceptable taste it was also quite filling. Greatly encouraged by his find, Gemree tentatively pulled a small handful of the green foliage from the side of the boat and held it to his nose. It had a slight scent of flowering shrubs, but was not unpleasant. He tugged experimentally at some strands with his teeth, and taking them into his mouth rolled them around his tongue. They actually tasted rather good. He took a large piece and chewed on it confidently. It was sweet, but not unlike broccoli. He leaned back and smiled. It seemed that the great problem of finding enough food to stay alive was solved.

He began to steer towards the Plantmass. Clearly he could not spend the days that lay ahead eating the boat that was hopefully, going to carry him through his journey. He laughed out loud, the very thought amused him. No, he must try to arrest the violent progress of his little craft, and cut enough supplies from the plantmass to last him until his journey's end, whenever that might be.

The manoeuvre proved to be easier said than done. It was no problem to get the boat close to the edge of the Plantmass, to lean over the side, and to grab at the unresisting surface. Unfortunately, his fingers simply closed over the plant's foliage which came away in his hands, resulting in his tumbling backwards in the now familiar jumble of arms and legs. He knew that the only way to stop the boat was to grab deep down to the network of roots. This, while being easy to envisage, presented certain difficulties in its accomplishment. After a number of futile and even comical attempts Gemree slumped down in the stern of the boat to try to solve the problem with logic rather than enthusiasm.

THE CAVERN

"The problems are," said Gemree to himself, "Number one – The roots lie a full arm's length beneath the surface of the foliage, that of course is why when I walk on the surface I sink down to my knees. The roots support me, but the foliage does not." He sat there holding the little finger of his left hand as he counted. "Number two," he took hold of the next finger. "The boat is travelling so fast, that before I can get my hand down to the roots, I have moved so far forward, that my arm has been pulled out again." He lay for some minutes pondering the problem, and then he simply stood up and took in his hand the plaited rope that was attached to the bow of the boat. A length of some ten feet still remained where he had sliced it with his sword. He tied the end tightly to his ankle and then pushed the tiller hard over to drive the little boat close to the Plantmass. As soon as the bow touched the edge, he leapt out of the boat and right into the green sponge. The speed with which he hit the surface was so great that he completely vanished from sight. The boat jerked to a sudden stop. Gemree emerged, like a pheonix arising. He was covered in green foliage, and his face was wreathed in smiles. He lay on his back, holding his leg, with the rope still tightly attached to his ankle, high in the air. His laughter echoed throughout the empty world.

The boat was once more making its speedy passage down the centre of the river. Gemree lolled in the stern, tiller under his arm and a huge pile of green foliage and creamy white roots by his side. He was content, as only a young man who was overcoming great problems can be. Not only had he satisfied his own need for food, but he had made provision for The Follower as well. He lay back and allowed himself to think about his next ordeal … the Cavern of the Bat.

The days that followed were strange, boring and yet enlightening days for Prince Gemree. Boring in that day followed day with nothing to do. Even the need to steer the little boat was one of choice and not necessity. He thought often of home, of King Pylon, of Pimm, of King Synod. He thought more often of the Cavern of The Bat, and of the Pit of Snakes. He thought of the beautiful maiden. He thought of the Great Knight of Rantoc, and the final Sacrifice to the Keeper of the Gates. He was not afraid, indeed his whole life had been a training for this day. His father had been a Knight of Arac, as had his father before him. A line stretching back to the Great King Synod himself. Gemree wondered why he of the twelve should have been chosen; he, the twelfth Knight, the Knight of the Orange and Blue, the least senior of them all. Was it a punishment? He thought not. Was it then the greatest honour that could ever be bestowed? Yes, yes, yes!

He thought about this strange land through which he was now travelling. It definitely wasn't Arac, for he had fallen through the very floor of the mountain to get here. It certainly wasn't

THE CAVERN

Sodah, because it was well known that Sodah was a land of barren and icy wastes, of days that were almost as dark as the nights. Everyone knew that the Prophecy of the True Word decreed that there would be a stranger, the Thirteenth Knight, who would come from another world. Was this the other world of which the Prophecy spoke? If so, where were the people? This land was warm, it was green, it was constantly bathed in sunlight. Gemree realised that there had been no night since he had arrived, yet his hunger and his thirsts told him that he had been travelling on this river for many days. But, where were the people? And when he came upon the Cavern of the Bat, would he have the courage and the skills to survive? He refused to think at length about the Pit of Snakes, one ordeal at a time was quite enough.

Many hours of each day were spent polishing his sword and shield – and praying for a skill to match his courage and for a courage to match his skill. Quietly, within his heart he knew that he would be equal to any tasks that lay before him.

It was, he estimated, the eleventh day. Since early morning he had detected a marked change in his surroundings. The rocky cliffs seemed lower now; in fact, their tops that until now had been invisible, could be clearly seen. Waterfalls no longer gushed and tumbled, he had seen the last of those on the third or fourth day. The Plantmass was now breaking up, and there were vast areas of water, with green islands floating like ice floes. Even the sun, which was still high in the sky, seemed to project less light and warmth, and had a thin, watery quality. As the day progressed, these manifestations increased and became more marked. Slowly, for the first time since his arrival in this strange land, a purple dusk began to fall. The dusk became a darkness. The darkness became a blackness. An inpenetrable blackness such as he had never known before. He held his hand before his eyes, he could feel his palm brushing his nose, but he could see nothing. With the blackness came a coldness that bit into his bones. At times, often, when at his station high in the Mountains of Synod with his squire Pimm, Gemree had known cold nights . But not like this, like pincers nipping his skin. Like icicles piercing his eyes. Like a hand of steel gripping his heart.

And then the fear started, a shuddering irrational fear. Many times he spoke, loudly, to himself. "It's dark and it's cold, but, I have been cold before, I have seen the dark before." He shivered, but the shiver was more than coldness, "I am not afraid" he told himself. But he was.

And then he heard it. Quietly, at first, as if from a million miles away. Not even a sound, more a feeling that a sound was there. He leaned forward as if that would make the hearing of it sharper. The air was being folded over, a soft and gentle whoosh, and then it was folded back again. The feeling of sound persisted for some time, and then it was a mere feeling no longer. Now the sound penetrated the ears as well as the mind. Now the sound became real, but with the reality the fear was lifted. Gemree, the twelfth Knight of Arac, the Knight of the Orange and Blue had an enemy that he could fight, an enemy that he could defeat.

The whoosh, whoosh, whoosh became louder and louder as it approached the little craft. Still total darkness pervaded the world around him. And then there were two pinpricks of light, two bright coals of fire, straight ahead and approaching. Gemree picked up a torch he had made from roots, and blessed the versatility of the wonderful plant. With sure and practised fingers despite the blackness, he took his tinder box from the pouch around his waist. There was a flash of flame, Gemree touched the browning foliage and it burst into bright light. He held his carefully prepared torch high and almost dropped it at the sight that met his eyes. The blackness was not caused by the night, the boat was drifting slowly through a huge cavern with high vaulted ceilings and water-dripping walls. The coals of fire that approached Gemree were the evil eyes of a creature from whom the worst of nightmares are made. It was a bat, and yet it could not be a bat. Its features were clear to see and had a malevolence beyond description. Each wing was the size of a Knight's cloak and folded over the body. As they opened, with a great whoosh of air, they revealed a long thin body with arms and legs that were skeletal and yet almost human. Gemree drew his sword, and with torch in one hand, and sword in the other, he stood in the gently rocking boat and waited for the attack from this creature in the Cavern of the Bat.

Chapter Eleven

The Bat

Gemree stood very still, his legs wide apart, bracing himself against the onslaught he felt sure was coming. He held the slow burning torch in his left hand, his arm outstretched to throw as much light as possible around the little boat. In his right hand he held his long broadsword, its blade, like the surface of the water beneath him, glinting in the flickering flame of the torch. The flames made shadows dance on the water and over the leafy hull of the boat. The huge creature, although a mere outline in the gloom, was an awesome sight. It seemed to hover in an almost upright position. It's skeletal, half human body was exposed, and then hidden from sight, as the huge wings unfolded, wide, and slowly, with a gentle rush of air. Then equally slowly they wrapped the body up again until only the rat-like head with its bright flame eyes could be seen above the top of the black, shroud-like wings. Gravity was denied in the moments that the wings were closed. The shape, like a roll of old cracked linoleum, maintained a stationary position some half a dozen feet above the surface of the water. And then, with a gentle 'whoosh' as the dank and heavy air was pushed aside, the wings would unfold once more and that macabre body would be exposed again, the thin legs dangling down like a stringless marionette.

By now all fear had left Gemree; at last he had an adversary he could see. Although it was probably the most fearsome he had ever encountered, it was still flesh and blood, and as such, vulnerable before his accomplished blade. Besides, although the creature was unpleasant to look at, Gemree could see nothing to the creature that could threaten his life. There were no cruel talons. In fact the arms seemed designed for no purpose other than to carry and to flap the huge wings. There were small hands with what appeared to be three fingers on each. Gemree could see no danger here. While the head and face was repugnant to behold, the mouth was small and carried no sharp teeth. From what Gemree could see, it seemed that there were no teeth at all. The head itself was sharply pointed, but not to the degree that it could pose a danger. The legs and feet, which hung loosely from the body, could best be likened to the legs of a frail old man. Certainly not a potential weapon to be feared. No, Gemree guessed that the greatest danger lay from those huge wings that, if he did not stay on his guard, would be capable of knocking him off balance, and even out of the boat. He widened his stride even more until he felt capable of withstanding any impact.

THE BAT

For a long time it seemed that the creature was content to hover, just a few feet in front of and above the boat. It hung there, folding and unfolding its wings in a gentle rhythm. Each movement was accompanied by that familiar 'whoosh' as the air was parted, and then rushed into to fill the hole left by the wings as they passed on. Gemree was used to battles where Knights, and sometimes fierce animals, would circle each other for many minutes, probing for weaknesses in each other. He used his time wisely, gauging, as closely as he could the distance the creature was from the bow of the boat, the height of its wings, the length of its body, and other such information the observance and remembrance of which, could in battle be the difference between victory and defeat. Subconsciously, and as a mark of his intense concentration, he counted the time between each flap of the wings. Whoosh-two-three-four-five-six-seven-eight-nine-ten Whoosh-two-three four-five-six-seven-eight-nine-ten. It was thanks to this quite subconscious act that he became aware of a slight and then more marked change of pace. Whoosh two three four five six seven eight Whoosh-two-three-four-five-six- seven-eight Whoosh-two-three-four-five-six-seven Whoosh-two-three-four-five-six-seven. The boat that had been sitting on the water as if on dry land, started to rock gently as the movement of air caused by the slightly faster moving wings caused little wavelets to run along underneath the hull. Gemree concentrated on the creature.

Except for the faster movement of the wings, it looked the same, although when folded, the wings were not wrapping the body up quite so completely as before. The legs still dangled helplessly below the body, and the head and eyes were unmoving. Gemree fancied that he saw an unexpected shadow pass across the water behind the creature, but he could easily have been mistaken.

Whoosh-two-three-four-five Whoosh-two-three-four-five. The little boat was moving more violently now and Gemree had to stretch out his torch arm to steady himself. The shadows danced wildly as he quickly dropped the level of the torch and then raised it high in the air again. Whoosh-two-three Whoosh-two-three Whoosh-two-three Whoosh-two-three. It was amazing, the creature still hovered motionless, hanging just a few feet above the surface. Yet the wings were really moving quite quickly now and Gemree could feel the movement of air, like a fresh breeze with each beat. The surface of the water was now becoming quite agitated and the boat bucked and rolled on its lumpy surface. Whoosh- two, Whoosh-two, Whoosh-two, Whoosh-two, Whoosh, Whoosh, Whoosh, Whoosh, Whoosh, Woosh, Wooosh, Wooosh, Woooosh, Wooooosh, Wooooooooosh, Woooooooooosh, Woooo-oooooooooooooooooooooosh, Wooooooooo ooooooooooooooooooooooooooooooooooo ooooosh!

THE BAT

Now Gemree could no longer differentiate between the beats, the water bubbled and seethed. The boat rose and fell, bucked and dived, rolled and rocked. It was impossible to stand. Water cascaded over the boat, leaving Gemree saturated. The torch was doused and again the all pervading blackness was relieved only by the piercing brightness of those evil eyes.

Gemree crouched in the bottom of the boat, his sword still securely held in his right hand. Instinctively he reached for his shield and slipped it on to his arm, moving it naturally in position to protect his chest and head. This action had been born of a lifetime's training. A moment later, he silently thanked his gods for the quality of that training. Almost at the instant that he brought the shield up to the 'protect' position, it was hit by a stream of white hot flame. The intensity of the heat blistered its surface. Its glare lit up the cavern and the creature with a brightness greater than an Aracian summers day. In that time-stopping moment, Gemree looked at the creature and saw twin tongues of flame fly from its malevolent eyes. Only his shield saved him from death. A glance at his gauntlets, now charred black, and the blistering skin of his arm beneath, showed him how close he had come to oblivion. He braced himself for a second fiery onslaught, but for the moment it did not come. He looked into the creature's eyes; they had been intensely bright and evil, they were now dim and lacklustre. Gemree knew that, for the moment at least, there was little or no danger of a further attack by flame. He also knew that, somehow, he must take the fight to the creature before it re-built the strength it needed to cover him in flame again. His shield, now twisted and bent, would not save him a second time. The wings had began to slow imperceptibly, and Gemree noticed that the creature was gradually turning away from the boat. Could it be, thought Gemree, that I have won, that he will now leave me in peace? But, even as he thought the words, he knew that the end could not be so inconclusive. He knew that he must defeat and kill the creature so that it posed no threat to The Follower.

The monstrous bat completed its turn. Gemree realised with a shock of horror, what the half-seen shadow had been. Now, in full display, was a tail the sight of which almost stopped Gemree in his tracks. It was at least a dozen feet in length and swished backwards and forwards across the water in deadly stokes that cut the water like a cleaver. As the creature completed its turn its back faced towards the boat. The tail suddenly lifted and lashed out with such force that its cracking sound seemed to split the air in two. The hard point of the tail struck the upright bow of the boat and sliced through as if it were paper. A large piece of the foliage and root dropped into the water and went spinning away into the darkness. Like a pendulum the tail swung back. There was another crack as the air split, and a portion of the boats bow, more than four feet across, vanished from sight. Gemree knew there was no time to lose. With the slowing of the wings, the waters had calmed and the boat now rocked only gently. This enabled Gemree to take a stance that braced him against the next slash from that evil tail. As he focused all his attention on the tail he saw it lift in preparation for its downward stroke. He raised his sword arm, and prepared to parry the blow. The long sinuous tail uncoiled like a whip lash. Gemree sensed, rather than saw its lethal descent as it curled towards him like the tongue of the dreaded mountain snake. Not for the first time, his life long training as a Knight, and his great fitness and agility had saved him from certain death. As he sensed that great tail with its wicked barbed end snaking towards him he dived frantically to his left, twisting sideways as he did so. He heard the tail swish through the air just inches away, exactly at the spot his head had been scant seconds before. The very instant that the creature realised that its prey had gone, the tail recoiled as quickly as it had uncoiled, and hung loosely beneath the huge black body.

During this exercise the wings had all but stopped beating. Now by the merest murmuring they kept the great body hovering, almost stationary, above and slightly in front of the little boat. Again, without warning, but with an almost imperceptible pre-movement that Gemree sensed, the tail spiralled down. This time Gemree was ready, and not only was he able to evade the flailing tail, but as it passed he brought his sword firmly down upon it. Then came Gemree's second surprise. He had expected to feel the broadswords sharp double-edged blade sink softly into flesh. Instead, the impact was as if his broadsword was being parried by another of equal strength. Like steel on steel. He realised that the tail was almost solid bone covered by thick reptilian scales. Notwithstanding, the creature was clearly capable of feeling pain, and Gemree's blow had caused it pain in some great measure. The creature re-acted with a scream that filled every corner of the great cavern in its intensity. A scream of such piercing anger, that Gemree was forced to put his hands tightly over his ears in an attempt to block out the sound. This time the tail did not whip lash back, but as the screech softened to a whimper, the tail was slowly and painfully withdrawn. The beast drew slowly away from the boat, as if to ensure that it was out of the range of a weapon capable of causing it pain in a way it had ever known.

For a very long time nothing happened. It was as if the huge, powerful, but slow witted creature had to allow all the facts to seep into its tiny reptilian brain and be absorbed slowly before any sort of alternate plan could be initiated.

Gemree was grateful for this short respite because it gave him time to gather his own senses. He relit the torch which had been extinguished as he had dived to avoid the first attack. In the light of the torch he inspected his sword. He found, to his amazement, that the force of the clash between sword and tail had been so violent that the hard tempered steel of the weapon that had once belonged to his father, had a huge tooth of metal missing. He smiled grimly realising that although his sword had been damaged by the great tail, unlike the creature, Gemree had experienced no pain. Judging by the Bat's unearthly scream, there was no way in the three worlds that the creature would be able to withstand a drawn-out onslaught between sword and tail. No, it was quite clear that the Bat would have to come up with a quite different plan of attack. Gemree allowed himself the optimism of thinking that perhaps he had now neutralized both the flame and the tail. All he could do now was wait, and hope that he would be equal to the next onslaught whatever form it took.

After a long time, by the light of the burning torch, Gemree became aware that the great wings had begun to move again. Slowly at first as, just like before, they seemed to fold and then unfold, pushing as they did so great draughts of air in front of them. The action gradually became more positive, and then slowly the attitude of the Bat's ugly body began to change. Imperceptably it moved from the vertical position to the horizontal. Like a huge storm cloud it began to slide, so slowly that its progress was almost unnoticable, over the boat. Soon the massive and now outstretched wings seemed to form a canopy that was a part of the vessel itself.

Gemree was still kneeling on the coarse matting that formed the floor of the boat. Now he found that he was looking up at the thin, skeletal, and frightening body of that loathsome creature, with its evil head and deep shining and malevolent eyes. He also became aware of the dusky decaying smell that was emitted from the creature. Like the smell of a long forgotten attic it seemed to fall from the body and hang in a mist just over Gemree's head. The Bat had this ability to hang in the air, almost motionless, without making any obvious movement with wings or body. This he did now, so close to the boat that had Gemree stood up he would undoubtedly have struck his head upon the leathered wings.

The bright, ruby red eyes moved slowly taking in every inch of the boat from stem to stern. Locking the images into its brain and their positions into its radar for future use. And then the eyes began to drill into Gemree himself. The thin black lips drew back from the sharp yellow teeth in an evil grin. Through the whole of this examination Gemree had remained quite still, and incapable of movement, as if mesmerised by those diabolic eyes. He could hear a small voice inside him telling him to attack while the creature was in such a vulnerably exposed position that no better chance would present itself. Yet he could not move. A lifetime's training for combat had been neutralized by a foe unlike any for which that training could ever have prepared him. "Gemree", this inner voice insisted, "strike now, or you will be defeated. Strike now, or your mission will be over. Strike now or Arac will surely fall." It was the voice of his long dead father. It was the voice of King Synod. It was the combined voices of his brother Knights.

Slowly the voices overcame the mesmeric effect of those compelling eyes. Memories of the green, lush, sweet smelling fields of Arac overcame the stench of decay and evil that hung over his head. In one instant he acted with instinct, and yet with great courage. In one movement he launched himself up from his knees. His head was immediately enveloped in one huge folding wing. Before he was blinded by its leathery folds he thrust the flaming torch into the creatures face, into the very eyes of that loathsome vision from hell. At the same time, he thrust his sword deeply into the resisting scales and gristly flesh of the obscene body. The jaws fell open and the creature emitted a banshee-like wail that made its earlier screams sound like the purring of a cat. The bright light of the eyes went out and a smell like that of burning rubber encompassed the boat. The sword had also done its work, and Gemree felt the drip of warm blood upon his hand, as it fell from the creature's wounded side.

As the shock of the assault lessened, the piercing wail became a long low throaty moan and the canopy that enveloped Gemree's head lifted and began to move slowly forward. The Bat reached the stern of the boat and drifted back into its now familiar upright position, a few feet to the rear of the boat. Now it floated no more than two feet above the surface of the water. Its eyes remained closed. Away from that satanic stare Gemree felt easier. The torch was now burning quite dimly following its brutal contact with the creature.

Gemree took this moment's respite, for he was sure that was all it was, to douse the flame. He tightly bound some more thick strands around the torch head, and relit it so that once more it burned with a bright and a comforting flame. He was in the uncomfortable situation of being quite powerless to take the battle to his adversary, separated as they were by air and water. Calmly he knelt on the bottom of the boat and concentrated with all his being on the hovering shape. It hung there menacingly before him, still emitting those low, throaty moans of pain and anger. The creature's next move took Gemree by complete surprise and suggested an intelligence far beyond that with which Gemree had credited it. Slowly Boney, for such had Gemree christened the creature, began to move its huge wings in that now familiar folding and unfolding motion. Faster and faster they beat. First the air stirred and then it was pushed towards Gemree like a light breeze that became a strong breeze, and then a violent wind. The noise of the wings invaded his mind. Wooo ossssshhhh! Woooosssssshhhhh! Wooooss-ssshhhhhh. The boat began to rock, and the water slapped against its sides. Gemree looked upwards at the creature. To his horror he saw that it was no longer stationary but was now moving at an ever increasing rate towards the boat. Somehow despite the obvious fact that the creature was moving forwards with each beat of its huge wings, the distance between it and the boat remained the same. The little craft was being pushed forward on waves of ever increasing size and force. Waves that were being generated on the water's surface by the motion of the wings alone. With each beat, the water's surface erupted with greater fury. Suddenly the boat was picked up by a wave, larger than any so far, and thrown forward. It was the first of a series of surges that was to mark the beginning of a boat ride the like of which Gemree would never know again. The boat gathered speed, slowly at first, but then more rapidly as the surface of the water began to dance to the beat of the great wings. The wings themselves beat faster and faster, until they became a mere blur of speed in the flame-lit blackness. In some miraculous way, Bony stayed the same distance from the boat, despite a wing speed that should have been propelling him through the air at a fantastic speed. One male-volent eye glared at Gemree, the other appeared to have been damaged beyond repair by Gemree's earlier attack.

The forward progress of the boat was now such that it was just impossible for Gemree to maintain his balance and still hold on to both the light giving torch, and his sword. So, returning his sword to its sheath, he plunged his hand through the Plantmass side of the boat and grabbed a firm hold on the root network below. Even so, he was tossed from side to side as the boat careered perilously through the tumbling waters. From side to side it was tossed, bouncing wildly from one wall of the cavern to the other. All the time the wings beat relentlessly. All this time the single eye glowed and glared evilly as the creature guided the boat and Gemree to what he felt sure was certain destruction.

By now all pretence at dignity, or even stability had gone. Angrily, he had flung the torch accurately but harmlessly at the creature. Now he lay full length in the bottom of the boat clinging on for dear life and waiting for his nightmare to end. The boat crashed into rocks and bounced high in the air as it careered off the towering granitelike walls of the cavern. It now seemed to Gemree that there was as much water in the boat as outside of it. Not for the first time he blessed the strange properties of the Plantmass, which gave such buoyancy and yet still allowed water to pass through it as if it did not exist. He knew that with any conventionally built boat, his journey would long since have ended with the boat a mass of flotsam and himself somewhere at the bottom of the black water. So that he would not be parted from this resilient craft, he had tied the leading rope tightly to his wrist. With his sword and his dagger now safely sheathed, he lay waiting for the ordeal to be over, and praying that when it was he would have just one more chance to revenge himself upon this evil creature. The end came in a most unexpected way.

Chapter 12

The Pit

Suddenly the little boat hesitated in its forward motion and hung suspended in mid air. Gemree could not imagine the cause of this strange phenomenon, but before he could make any move his stomach lurched violently as the boat slowly turned turtle in the air and began to fall. As it gathered speed Gemree was conscious of a solid curtain of water to his side, and pitch blackness below. He was to discover later that the river that he had been following for so long had suddenly plunged into a huge black void, and he had been carried over the waterfall at breakneck speed. The fall felt interminable. Some-how he managed to retain his double handed grip. As the boat turned and twisted on its downward path he found himself hanging on for dear life. One moment he was hanging crazily below the boat, the next, they both turned in the air, and he was being bruised and battered, as the speed of the fall forced him against the coarse floor matting.

They hit the water with such a crash that he was forced to let go of his vice like grip. In that moment he was plunging straight down into a black, and seemingly bottomless, water-filled pit. Suddenly and very painfully he jerked to a halt. It was not until later that he realized that the rope which he had tied to his wrist had saved his life. He had hit the water first, and then the boat followed him in hitting the surface with a thunderous crash.

The speed of its fall, together with the momentum of Gemree's descent, had forced the boat to follow him down, down, into the cold, black, depths. Fortunately the little craft's natural buoyancy arrested its downward plunge within seconds, and it had bobbed up to the surface again just like a cork. It was this upward motion that had caused the shoulder wrenching jerk that had stopped Gemree, as the rope, still attached to the boat's bow, had reached its limit. The pain that shot through his arm was excruciating but it was a small price to pay for being saved from a very cold and watery grave. With his lungs bursting he kicked upwards and hauling on the rope, began to make his way with a half pulling, half swimming motion, to the surface.

Just as he thought he could hold out no longer, his head broke through into the dank and fetid, but at that moment, sweet, sweet air. Clinging to the side of the upturned boat, he gratefully dragged air into his tortured lungs.

As his breathing slowed down to normal he tried to look around. He could see nothing, except that is a pinprick of bright red light, high above his head. As he watched it became larger.

He also became conscious of a deep thumping sound, slow and very low. It took but a few seconds for his greatest horror to be realized. It was not a light that he saw, but the one remaining and baleful eye of the creature Boney. Thump, thump, thump. He heard the awful sound of its wings as they beat slowly and precisely to allow the creature to descend carefully into the pit where it could ensure that Gemree was destroyed for ever.

He thought fast; he remembered the lethal accuracy of the fiendish tail and knew that he must have protection from its attack. Hauling upon the rope around his wrist, he pulled the little boat closer to him. Feeling carefully with his hand he realised that the boat had actually hit the water the wrong way up. It was therefore now floating upside down. At that moment there was a fearsome crack like thunder and the water alongside Gemree's head erupted. He knew it was the vicious tail beginning its final wicked work of destruction. He blessed the fact that the boat had landed the way it had. Quickly he ducked under the water, and, pulling himself forward on the rope, re-surfaced under the boat. As he had guessed there was a large airspace between the water's surface and the bottom of the boat, now about three feet above his head. It was pitch black, but he heaved a great sigh of relief with the knowledge that, for the moment at least, he was safe. He was aware that he would find it difficult to influence the outcome of the battle from his present position, but, at least he had given himself time to plan his next move. Distantly he could hear the thrashing sound of the tail as it crashed, sometimes against the waters surface, and sometimes against the bottom of the boat itself. It was clear to him that if he were to survive, and more importantly be able to clear the way for The Follower, he must take the battle to the creature in such a way as to emerge victorious. It was a tall order, but an order that not only must he obey, but that he must obey successfully. He cleared his mind of all extraneous matters and began to concentrate totally upon the immense task before him.

Holding on to the underside of the boat, and with his legs dangling in the water below him, he took stock of his situation.

1. He was, effectively, blind in that unforgiving blackness that was darker than the night itself. On the other hand, to the creature with its uncanny radar, it was as if it was the brightest of days. The first advantage definitely belonged to Boney.

2. He had lost both the torch and his shield, but as fortune would have it his sword and his dagger were both safely sheathed. He thanked providence for giving him the foresight not to simply leave them lying on the floor of the boat. This gave him two very effective weapons against Boney's tail. A tail that, while being able to inflict great damage, was, as Gemree had so ably proved, capable of feeling great pain. The

advantages in the weapon department belonged, most definitely he decided, with him.

3. He had the cover and the protection of the boat. The creature had no protection beyond the all enveloping blackness. Gemree decided that here was another advantage most certainly favouring him.

4. Finally, the creature had to keep himself airborne in what appeared to be a very re-stricted space. As far as Gemree knew, bats could not swim. Assuming that such was the case with his friend Boney, here was not just an advantage but a definite weakness. It was to exploit this weakness that Gemree began to conceive a plan.

The question was, how to get the creature down to the water's surface? He was particularly aware that he could see nothing but the creature's single eye as the great black shape simply melted into the greater blackness that surrounded him. He must therefore make that evil pinpoint of light the focus around which to conduct the most important fight of his young and Knightly life. As he carefully considered all of the possible options, a plan began to form in his mind. With a smile on his lips he drew his dagger carefully out of the sheath at his belt. He began to hack away at the Plantmass that formed the bottom of the boat, and which now floated just a short distance above his head. He kept the leading rope tied tightly to his wrist so that there was no danger of the little boat drifting away from him, if, during the second part of his plan he should find himself parting company with the craft. So prepared he began to work diligently at his task.

It was a surprisingly short time before Gemree had succeeded in carving a hole through the tough woven root flooring and into the hull. He made the hole just large enough for him to squeeze his slim body through and then began to hack away at the hull itself. Soon he could feel the draught of air caused by the beating of the huge wings, and he knew that he had successfully completed his job.

All the time he had been working he had been listening carefully to the ever quickening thrashing of the tail upon the water's surface as the creature strove vainly to make contact with its adversary. But more than this, Gemree had also been aware of another sound, as of human frustration, a low moan rose from the creature's throat and became more intense with every passing moment as it failed to find its enemy in the cold black water. Gemree decided that he must be prepared to take advantage of this frustration. His plan entailed a colossal risk, but he knew that it was a risk he could not shirk. Slowly and carefully he pulled himself upwards through the hole that he had cut in the hull until he was able to lie, face up, on the bottom of the upturned boat. He held his dagger in his left hand, and his right hand was free. His sword lay in a now unclasped sheath, secure, but ready. As if by magic the creature seemed to sense his presence. Like a whiplash, the tail thrashed unmercifully across his legs with a blinding flash of pain that made him cry out in agony. The cry, the only one that Gemree determined he would make, mingled with a shriek of triumph that replaced the low moan that had been accompanying the creature's, until now, fruitless search. A second time the tail cracked down, this time flailing across Gemree's body, first his thighs, and then on an almost instantaneous return journey across his stomach. Biting back a cry of pain, he secured his grip upon his dagger, and prepared for the next bone-shaking assault. The creature had no such reticence, and the screech that left that deformed body appeared to be one of pure joy. Almost a victory scream as it man-oeuvred itself for a final attack, carefully gauging direction and distance for the killing blow.

Gemree concentrated all of his senses on the black shape above him and waited for this fourth attack. He had endured the first three without resistance because he had had to learn their pattern. His plan required him to grab that vicious tail in its flight. Like a blind man he had to rely on his sense of hearing, his sense of touch and even his sense of smell to achieve this end. His intense concentration had not been in vain. He had noticed, just before the tail began its downward journey, the creature's sharp intake of breath.

A sharp, whistling sound, almost as if it needed this sound to give momentum to the tail as it coiled tightly before unleashing its power and its venom. As the tail was coiled there had been the merest rustling sound as it had brushed against the dry, leathery texture of the malformed body. Gemree had had time to count to just three from that almost inaudible rustle until the sharp crack of the tail and instantaneous flame of pain across his flesh. After the pain a count of just two seconds, and the tail had been withdrawn.

These were to be the vital two seconds that, if he were successful, would spell the destruction of the creature. Gemree had to believe that the final blow would be aimed at his throat, and following that belief he placed his right hand across his neck with the hand open, as if preparing to catch a ball. He had unfastened the rope from his wrist and fashioned a small noose with an easy running slip knot in the end. He stuck his dagger back in his belt, and with the noose held loosely in his left hand he lay on his back straining his ears into the darkness.

There it was, the sharp whistling intake of breath, and then the gentle rustling as the tail coiled. One. Two. Three. First the crack, and then immediately the pain, but not as the creature would have had it across Gemree's throat, but across his gauntleted and protected hand. As the pain burnt through the strong leather of the gauntlet Gemree closed his fingers. One, he dropped the noose over the pointed tail so that it slipped safely over the barbed end. Two, CRACK -the tail began whiplash back to its coiled position. Suddenly Gemree found himself clinging on for dear life as the little boat lurched on to its side. He dug his hands deeply into the Plantmass until they closed over the network of tough roots. The tail, restricted in its return to its sinister body, began to thrash from side to side as it tried to shake off the rope that held it. The boat rocked violently as it did so.

Gemree was quite convinced that he would have to let go and take his chances in the cold water. The movement became more and more violent, the creature more and more agitated, like a whale caught by a harpoon.

Again it began to make the unearthly, banshee wail, that Gemree had first heard when he had struck the tail with his sword. As its efforts became more frenzied, the inhuman sound became louder and louder and of a higher and higher pitch. It was an assault on his eardrums that was almost more painful than the attack upon his body. Eventually, both the motion and the sound lessened as the creature began to tire. Gemree waited until the boat was once more reasonably stable, and then, standing up on the hull he proceeded to put the second part of his plan into operation.

Using the tail, which now flapped feebly, to steady him, he withdrew his sword from its sheath. The creature sensed the movement and once more started to thrash that once lethal tail, wildly from side to side. Gemree locked his fingers together, and hung on for dear life. His feet were torn from the bottom of the boat, and he was lashed backwards and forwards out over the surface of the water. If he had fallen at that moment he would have met a death more terrible than his worst imaginings. Slowly the creature's tail stopped its flailing, and again hung limply. Gemree regained his footing. He allowed his breathing to slow and his mind to once more gain control of his body. Imperceptibly the great wings began to slow in their beat, and Gemree knew that the moment for him to attack had come.

Standing upright, his head was no more than two or three feet below the creature's dangling feet. By lifting his arm he could grasp its dry and leathery legs with ease. This he now did and his grip resulted in another flurry of activity. A further thrashing of the tail, a kicking of the bony feet, and a desperate flapping of the wings. However, all the force and the fury appeared to have left the creature as the weight of the boat now firmly tied to its tail, began to take its toll. Gemree drew his sword, he knew that the moment had come. What he now planned to do was dangerous in the extreme, and, had he known the horror which now lurked below the surface of that unfriendly water, he would never have had the courage to take the gamble that he did. Fortunately he was blissfully unaware and expected, at worst, a very unpleasant ducking. With his sword extended in his right hand, and his left tightly gripping the creature's leg, he threw himself backwards so that the whole of his dead weight was added to the weight of the boat.

The effect was startling. Boney, tired to the point of exhaustion, simply gave up, and fell on Gemree. He found himself lying in a heap on the upturned hull, struggling to find air. The great weight of the hideous thing, with its huge wings, and its odious little body, enveloped him. The face of the creature was inches from his, the one remaining eye alive with malevolence and hate. The yellow teeth were drawn back in the rat like jaw, and from the open mouth came a fetid smell that almost made Gemree retch. The great wings draped lifelessly over the boat and dragged in the water. There was a curious bubbling in the water which seemed to come from where the wings lay touching its surface. The creature twisted and moaned as if in pain. Once or twice it tried to lift its wings out of the water below, but the effort was too much. It was clear that at last, the creature's great strength was all but spent. Gemree had no room to manoeuvre because of the weight upon him. His sword arm was twisted underneath one of the huge wings, and try as he might, he was quite unable to lift it. He had let go of the creature's leg, and his own left hand was now pressed against its chest in an effort to keep those sharp and yellow teeth away from his throat. The creature was a dead weight, and as Gemree looked into its single eye it seemed that it had accepted its defeat, but, was not prepared to die alone. Aware that it needed to do nothing but lie there to render Gemree quite helpless, it now concentrated all of its efforts in forcing its rotting but lethal teeth into a position where they could close around Gemree's unprotected throat. With an unexpected, and as a result, successful move, the creature suddenly darted its head forward. The movement was so sudden that Gemree was completely taken by surprise. He felt a red-hot lance of pain as the jagged icicles of the creature's teeth sank deeply into the flesh of his cheek. He felt warm blood on his hand, which was still around the creatures throat. Suddenly the verminous head was thrown back. He almost lost consciousness as those razor sharp teeth, which had remained tightly locked over the flesh of his cheek, tore a huge portion of that flesh away from his face. The pain was beyond description and Gemree felt the blood, which had dribbled over his neck, now gush over his chin and bring him to the point of nausea. He could feel the head now forcing its way downwards towards his throat. Through a pain muddled haze he knew that if those teeth succeeded in closing over his throat, then, not only would it be the end for him, but for The Follower, and for his beloved Arac.

The head darted down again and it was only at the very last minute that Gemree managed to deflect it from his neck.

The teeth closed once more over the already mutilated cheek. The jaws locked in an unrelenting grip. With what must have been the last reserves of its strength, the creature began to shake his head from side to side. Pillars of pain shot through the whole of Gemree's body, and although emanating from his shattered cheek, it now seemed to invade every corner of his body. He could hear his cheek bones splintering, and he knew that by now half his face was gone. He had lost so much blood that his own strength was ebbing fast, and for the first time he began to face the prospect of defeat. In his mind he saw King Pylon, smiling at him. He remembered dear Pimm - did any man have a truer servant or a greater friend. The village in which he was born, with its green fields and its tumbling blue waters, danced before his eyes. He could see the people, his people, the people of Arac, who were relying upon him.

"I will not die," said Gemree softly, and then in a shout that startled the creature into stillness, "I WILL NOT DIIIEEEE!"

He looked into the creature's single eye, and the triumph that had been there just a moment before began to fade. The pain, like searing torches was now so much beyond bearing that it belonged to somebody else. In a complete trance, moving by instinct and will alone, Gemree removed his hand from the creature's breast, "let him do his worst" he thought,

Slowly, inch by inch, he slid his hand down to his belt and his fingers closed over the hilt of his dagger. He had little movement, and no knowledge at all of the creature's anatomy. Did it have a heart? Where were its vital organs? Even through the confusion of pain, he knew that he would only have one chance. If he made a mistake now, it would be the last he ever made. In that instant he knew what his target must be. The one remaining eye. The window of the creature's wicked and twisted soul. The very gateway to its reptilian brain. Gradually he slid his left hand, and the dagger, up his body until it lay beside his head. Carefully he turned the blade in his hand until the hilt rested comfortably in his palm. The pain now washed over him in huge waves as the creature once more began to toss its head from side to side like a dog with a bone. It was now, or it was never. He forced himself to concentrate, to count the beat as the head jerked first left, two three four, and then right two three four.....left, two three four, right two. Gemree arched his back and thrust his left hand upwards with all the force that his bunched and desperate muscles could muster. The accuracy of that blade must have been guided by some other hand. Unerringly, the long thin blade struck the centre of that bright and evil light that exploded - and then darkened in that same instant. The end was almost an anti-climax. The creature let out one heart rending cry, loosed its grip on Gemree's cheek, and died, quietly, no thrashing, no involuntary spasms. One moment it was alive and evil, and life threatening, the next it was no more. All of its weight now lay upon Gemree, but, relieved of the searing pain, he at last lapsed into the luxury of unconsciousness.

THE THIRTEENTH KNIGHT

He had no way of knowing how long he had laid there. He came to, shivering with the cold, and he guessed at his massive loss of blood. He managed to lift his hand to the hole that had once been the left side of his face. Blood no longer flowed, as nature had administered its own medicine and congealed the mess around the wound. He began to press against the inert body of the creature. It was unresisting, but, although a long and difficult job, he eventually managed to get sufficient leverage with both his arms and his legs to tip the huge body off the boat and into the water below.

What happened next was the stuff of nightmares. The water became a seething, bubbling, writhing mass and Gemree, with eyes at last becoming accustomed to the all pervading, blackness, was able to make out a scene from the very depths of hell. Twisting, writhing serpents fell upon his late and unlamented adversary. In the merest of moments they had reduced that huge carcass to — to nothing at all. For a long time after those demonic shapes had slid below the water and the surface was once more calm and untroubled, Gemree lay there looking with horror stricken eyes at the occasional ripple or bubble. He was not remembering the helter skelter dash in the little boat. He was not remembering the stomach lurching descent over the waterfall. He was not even remembering the fight for life with the great bat, the fight he had so nearly lost.

THE PIT

He was remembering hitting the black water. He was remembering plunging down into those dark, unfriendly depths. He was remembering those long minutes underneath the boat, while he cut the hole through the hull, before he climbed up to the safety of the boat's bottom. He was remembering his legs dangling there, unprotected in the icy water. Dangling, while those nightmares from hell were rising upwards from the bottom of the pit.

Chapter 13

Trueworld

Gemree slept. It was a remarkably untroubled sleep. A sleep without dreams. He awoke cold but refreshed, and lay for a long time thinking about his predicament. More particularly he was wondering how he could make the passage safe for The Follower .

He had survived the fall through the golden waterfalls on to the Plantmass. He could take no credit for that, and could only hope that, as King Synod had guided him into Trueworld, so he would guide The Follower. From the Plantmass he had given pointers as to the way that must be followed. He had also provided the means to follow that way. The River flowed naturally to its destination and he had taken steps to ensure that The Follower would not be without food for the journey. The river would take The Follower into the darkness of the Cavern, and he had left torches so that The Follower would have light. The Bat was dead and would pose no threat – and so The Follower's way to this dreadful place, The Pit of Snakes was cleared of all danger. Two things now caused Gemree grave concern. First, would The Follower survive a fall into the Pit as he had done? Second, if he did, what chance would he have when confronted by that contorted mass of evil that lived beneath the surface of the black water. It had become obvious to him that these frightening creatures lay at the bottom of this awful place only until the surface of the water was disturbed.

Then they rose to the surface to kill and devour their victim. Thanks to the rope that he had tied to his wrist he had been able to pull himself quickly to the surface, and then climb on to the hull of the boat. Even now he broke into a cold sweat at the thought of how close he must have come to death, and again saw his legs dangling deeply into the water as he had worked on carving a hole in the boat's hull. He shook himself back to the moment. It was clear that the creatures' appetites had been satiated by the great beast they had devoured, and so he felt that, for the moment he was safe. But what of The Follower? He would not see the need to tie himself to the boat, and with no other meal presented to them, the snakes and serpents would show him no mercy. He realized anew that his job here was far from done, and with that thought in his mind, again he slept.

He had no way of knowing how much time had elapsed since he had closed his eyes. He did know that he was very hungry and very thirsty and that neither craving would be satisfied until he had escaped from this dreadful pit. He drew his large broadsword, and using the blade as a paddle he began to propel himself across the surface of the water. He paddled away from the sound of the falling water that signified the sheer face of rock leading upwards towards the Cavern of the Bat. He could make out dim shapes, and his heart missed a beat at the thought that they were some awful creatures, as yet unseen. As he got closer they, thankfully, turned into large, and randomly placed, boulders. These stones seemed to mark the edge of the Pit, which, surprisingly, was no more that 50 feet across. He saw that while the walls behind him were sheer, those ahead were made up of many such irregularly shaped rocks and boulders. They sloped gently upwards almost forming a natural staircase into the blackness. He tied the little boat, still floating upside down, to a protruding rock and began to climb upwards. The way was easy and it took but a few moments to reach a spot opposite to where the waters from the cavern crashed over the precipice and down into the Pit. He was amazed to note that the distance from where he stood to the opposite wall was hardly more than 15 feet. This meant that the pit was shaped like an inverted funnel, narrow at its head and widening to three times its width at its base. From somewhere above him and to his right he could hear the sound of tumbling water as it fell to form a fast moving, but shallow stream just below his feet. It was obvious to him that once, the river down which he had travelled, had run an uninterrupted course across the point where this chasm, this fissure in the rock that was the Pit, now lay. At some time past perhaps an earthquake or perhaps a fault in the mountain's floor, had split the rocks apart and formed the deep black hole at the bottom of which the snakes now bred, and into which the river carried its unwary travellers.

If he could somehow re-instate the original course of the river, then The Follower need fear neither the Cavern nor the Pit, but could float serenely on the meadow of the beautiful maiden. He applied his mind to the problem. Somehow, that small gap of just 15 or so feet needed to be bridged in a manner that would enable the water to once more flow across it. The flow need not be fast, nor the depth great. What he needed were the materials to build a simple aqueduct, such as the one that carried the River Titch across the narrow gorge outside his own village in his beloved Arac. How would he find such materials stumbling about in the half light of the dark unfriendly place? Half light, it was true. Where there had been total blackness there was now definite lightening. He looked around, and when his eyes followed the direction in which the stream flowed it was clear that the darkness was less acute. There was a grey tinge to the blackness, which suggested far off daylight. He knew that it was only in the friendliness of the sunshine that he could find the means to fulfil his task, and enjoy the warmth that might go some way to repairing his weary and bruised body and mutilated face. He stepped down into the water and with long strides set out in the direction of the sun.

He walked for many hours. He walked through boredom. He walked through exhaustion. He walked through pain. His eyes stared unwaveringly at the ever increasing area of greyness that eventually became a circle of light. As he progressed the circle began to fade from his sight, and he was almost thrown into a state of panic. Then, he remembered that outside this wretched and perpetual darkness, there was a world where the sun rose and brought with it warmth and light, but where it also set to bring the night. His circle of light had disappeared for the very best of reasons, outside in the beauty of Trueworld night had fallen. He stepped out of the stream and finding himself a dry place between two large rocks, he lay down and fell instantly asleep. He dreamed of bright sunlight, of blue rivers, and he dreamed of a beautiful maiden.

When he opened his eyes, they fell upon a circle of bright yellow which signified that the sun was already high in the sky. He leapt up, and, stepping back into the water started to run towards the light in a fast though stumbling step. And then he was there, bursting into a yellow and blue wonderland such as he had not seen since before he set off with Pimm to his station high in the Synod mountains. His eyes, his mind and his heart drank in the scene before him. The stream had emerged from the mountain twenty or so feet above a broad and deep blue river into which it now gently tumbled. The river wound its way around the base of the mountain – flowing slowly away to the south. On the other side of the river immediately opposite to where he stood, was a meadow of yellow and gold grasses, filled with wild flowers of every conceivable colour. Down to the left, and some hundreds of yards away from the river bank, which itself abounded in bull-rushes and tall waving reeds, was an orchard full of trees heavy laden with fruit of all descriptions. Eventually the orchard thickened out The nature of the trees changed, and soon gave way to a deep green forest. From the river bank to the orchard, bounded on the right by the beautiful meadow, was a field of tall golden corn. The ears were full and heavy, and the tall stalks swayed gently backwards and forwards in the soft breeze. As if this picture needed enhancement, birds hovered and plummeted in the air. Huge dragonflies with silver blue bodies and a blur of wings darted from reed flower to reed flower. On the surface of the river busy little ducks fussed this way and that, while majestic swans floated lazily, viewing the world with disdain as their heads slowly turned from side to side at the top of their graceful, curving necks. If the scene of Gemree's past days had been conceived and carved in hell, then this was surely a scene that had been created and painted in heaven.

For many minutes he drank in this unbelievable beauty then, with a cry of pure joy, and just knowing that no dangers could lurk beneath the surface of this placid river, he dived in and swam gratefully through the warm clear water. Like a small child he pulled himself onto the bank and ran through the waving grass laughing joyously as he went. He ran through the tall and swaying corn into the orchard, where he dashed from tree to tree, jumping high to pick the fruit that almost fell from the boughs. He ate with relish and at last, with appetite satisfied, he fell upon the soft green grass beneath a huge damson tree and allowed the gentle warmth of the bright yellow sun to caress him into a deep sleep.

He slept a sleep such as he had never known. A sleep full of wonderful dreams and happy memories. A sleep of peace. A sleep of such restorative qualities that it could only have been driven by magic. When he awoke his whole body felt charged with a vitality and a strength beyond anything of which he was familiar. His skin glowed and his muscles rippled. Involuntarily he put his hand to his mutilated face, the skin was smooth and clear. All signs of the wound had gone. He ran to the very edge of the river bank and peered over into the calm water. Looking back was a young man who glowed with health, who bore no wounds, no signs of struggle or hardship. He blessed the magic of this wonderful place and with a light heart set about gathering the materials that would enable him to complete his self given task.

He strode through the orchard and to the

point where the river bent towards the forest and the trees began to thicken. He walked back and forth until he found what he sought. A tall, straight, yet young tree, thin in its girth, which could be cut down by patient application of his broadsword. He cut the sign of Arac upon its trunk. He repeated this process until he had marked six such trees. And then began the slow painstaking job of bringing them to the ground. For many hours he carefully hacked at their base with his sword. It was slow and demanding work, but, eventually he had the six trees, each ramrod straight and some 25 feet in length lying side by side on the river's bank. Satisfied with his work he then began to walk up and down the river bank gathering armfuls of bullrushes and reeds and dropping them by the side of the small trees. After some while a small mountain of these resilient water plants lay on the bank. Yet, even now he was not done . For the remaining daylight hours he gathered and carried to the river bank sheaths of corn which he laid beside the others. He felt that his day had been well spent, and lay with his back against the logs and settled down to await another glorious sunrise.

He awoke with the sun, once more refreshed by this magical place. He bathed in the dawn-cool water, and then walked through the orchard and ate his fill of dew laden fruits. Soon he was ready to work. Sitting cross-legged on the river bank, the sun beating pleasantly upon his back, he began a labour that was to take him many blister making hours to complete. First he took the long yellow stalks of corn and began to weave them, five or six thick, into single long, tough strands. Each cleverly spliced to the next. Eventually he had an unbroken rope of corn that lay along the bank stretching for over 100 yards. By this time the sun was well into the afternoon sky and Gemree stretched and walked to the orchard for more of the delicious fruit. His labours for the first day were done.

On the second day he took the young trees, and along the full length of the first he cut deep notches with his dagger, at intervals of less than two feet. On the first tree the notches were on one side only. On the second tree there were twice as many notches, cut to each side of the trunk at identical intervals to the first. The third tree was cut as the first, and then the trunk was rolled over so that the notches lay at the bottom. Having finished this, he placed the trees, one on the other. The notches on the top and bottom trunks lined up with those on the centre log. The deep cuts matched each other perfectly. He then passed the corn rope through the notches along his three trees and bound the trunks tightly together. When he had finished, he began again with the other three trees, repeating the process on the other side. Eventually he had all the logs strapped firmly together and placed about six feet from each other. Dusk was falling by the time he had completed the labours of his second day. The third day was as the first. Sitting cross-legged on the bank he began, with the rising of the sun, to weave the huge pile of bullrushes and reeds into a long wide cloth, firm to the touch, and some ten feet wide and twenty-five feet long. When it was completed he began the laborious job of securing this tough matting to the gap between the logs, tying loose ends left for the purpose tightly into the corn stalk rope that held the logs together. When this was done he walked to the orchard and cut down many long thin but strong branches. These he fixed securely between the two log walls. At last he was able to turn the whole thing over, and for the first time, its shape and its purpose became obvious. The structure was some twenty-five feet long, with two timber sides each around four feet high. The width of the structure was about six feet, and took the form of an open-ended box. The bottom of the box was now formed by a strong bulrush and reed matting resting on a criss cross of branches for added strength. The sun had by now gone down, and so ended his labours for the third day. He met the fourth day with great happiness in the knowledge that his job was all but done. Wading into the water he scooped up a double handful of thick grey mud and began to smooth it thickly over the sides and base. All day long he scooped up the mud from under the blue waters and patted it and smoothed it over the structure. By late afternoon it was completed. The oldest form of water proofing known to man, puddled clay. He stood back and gazed proudly at the aqueduct that would span the Pit and bring The Follower safely to the wonders of Trueworld. And so his work for the fourth day was completed. On the fifth day he could do nothing, as the newly built aqueduct had to dry in the warm sun. With the day stretching luxuriously before him he awoke early, and set out to explore the paradise that was Trueworld. He knew that he must fill his mind and his soul with it's beauty before venturing again, as he must, to the darkness and evil of the inner mountain.

Not for the first time he let his mind play back his dream, the dream that told him of the Ordeals that he must still face. He remembered the awfulness, now thankfully behind him, of the Cavern of the Bat and the Pit of Snakes. He smiled as he recalled that in the next part of his dream he had met a beautiful maiden with the golden hair, that was one part of his Ordeals that he could approach with joy and enthusiasm. How would he meet her? Would he round a bend in the river to see her standing there waiting? Would he hear her calling him from a great distance? Would she simply appear like a magical apparition from out of a mystical haze? He was now striding boldly along a straight stretch of the river. Because of the auto suggestion in which he had been indulging, he allowed himself to believe that it was beyond that very bend that his dream, that the vision of loveliness, so clearly re-membered from his dream, would appear. He began to quicken his stride, first to a jog and then to an easy run, his long legs carrying him swiftly across the ground. Dimly he became aware of a distant sound that seemed to come from behind him and to his left, from the forest of tall trees, the edge of which appeared to follow every curve of the river's bank. At first he ignored it, but it became gradually louder and more insistent. A noise like the beating of a drum. He slowed again to walking pace and glanced over his left shoulder from where the sound seemed to come. What he saw made his mouth drop open in speechless amazement.

Just inside the line of trees, on the edge of the meadow galloped the most magnificent horse that he had ever seen. It was white, but such a description does no justice to a colour that shone and sparkled in the sunlight. It was white, because there is no colour that has silver flecks dancing on its surface. No colour that reflects the hints of ice cold blues and translucent golden tints. And yet, these colours were moving colours that caught the reflected light as the galloping muscles rippled. The long soft mane flew behind the magnificent animal like the proud pennant of a sailing ship bending before the wind. The horse veered away from its path which was running parallel to, though slightly behind Gemree's own, and, without slowing its pace set a diagonal course that would bring it to the very place where he stood, now rooted to the spot, in silent awe of the glorious animal. As the horse got close it slowed, first to a canter and then to a trot.

Finally it came alongside Gemree and stood patiently before him nuzzling his outstretched hand. Gemree looked around, he appeared to be the only person in the world on that wonderful sunny day. He alone, a Knight in soft and silver armour, he alone, and a magnificent white stallion that stood fully fourteen hands high. It was the stuff of which fairy tales are made.

The horse kept pushing its head against his hand. He patted its nose lovingly, in the way of a man who knows and loves horses. He thought fondly of his own faithful mount, White Heart, whom he had left grazing on the banks of the pool in which sat The Saddlestone. As he stroked the animal's broad back he became obsessed with the need to ride this wonderful creature, to feel the power of those bulging muscles beneath his legs. This obsession became intolerable, until he could think of nothing else. And, then, in a moment, he leapt athletically on to the horse's back. He revelled in that never forgotten feeling as the great animal reared up on its hind legs, pawing the air in front of it. Gemree clung to his mane and shouted, "Go, my lovely, let us gallop like the wind, you and I." With a loud shout of joy from the man, and a whinny of triumph from the animal, the hooves crashed down onto the ground, and a flight began. And a flight it almost was, so swiftly and surely did that white wonder fly over the ground. Swifter than the wind. Surer than the river itself in its self knowledge.

It melted around trees that appeared in its

path. It flew over hedgerows and rocks with jumps that put it on a level with the birds. The wind sent the milky mane flying behind it.

In his exhilaration Gemree knew no fear, his thighs and his calves firmly gripped the creature's broad body. The fingers of his right hand dug into the animal's soft mane while his left arm punched the air with the pure joy. The joy of a poetry of motion and movement that is seen but once in ten lifetimes, and experienced once in a thousand.

The miles disappeared beneath those flying hooves. The meadows changed to cornfields. The cornfields turned to forests, and the forests to pastures. The pastures turned to hillsides, and the hillsides back to cornfields. The world fled beneath those hooves, but still the horse galloped as if the joy of heaven was in its heart, and the demons of hell upon its tail. Gemree had no conception of time, no conception of distance. The past merged with the present and the present merged with the future. And then, ahead, there was a dot; the dot became a shape, the shape became a horse. A horse as black as midnight. A horse that galloped as Gemree's mount galloped, that charged towards him as if for a meeting arranged by destiny. He watched as the midnight beauty drew closer and closer. His hand fell to the hilt of his sword, he knew not who he was about to face, but this land would not surprise him again. But it did. The two animals were now little more than 400 yards apart, and he could now see clearly that the black horse had a rider. The rider was the one he had so longed to see, but who, in the thrill of the gallop had been forgotten. Despite the great speed of the approaching horse a beautiful maiden, in white flowing gown and with golden flowing hair, sat easily, side saddle upon the black beauty. She moved with the horse as if they were just one flesh. Her head was thrown back in laughter, and her teeth, shining white as jewels, sparkled in the sunlight. At full gallop the horses, now no more than a few yards apart, approached each other, and then, they stopped. No vigorous skidding of hooves as they tried to gain purchase on the soft ground. No bone wrenching, muscle twisting jerk as they slithered to a halt, with the helpless riders trying to carry on their journeys alone. The horses simply stopped, without fuss, without effort. One moment they were at breakneck gallop, the next they were quietly nuzzling against each other, before putting their heads to the ground to tear off great clumps of the sweet grass that lay beneath their feet.

Gemree raised his hand at the start of a bow to this beautiful apparition, but, before he could do anything she spoke. "My Lord Gemree – I knew you would survive. Welcome to Trueworld, my name is Tashka, I am The Lady of Micrascar." Gemree did not speak. He had been overcome by her beauty; now he was bewitched by a voice that sounded like the sweetest music he had ever heard.

"I hope you like your horse, he is called Swift-sure, and will help you through the ordeals to come. Swiftsure is the brother of Dark Star. Together they have more speed, more grace, and more love than any in the Three Worlds."

Gemree still sat speechlessly upon the horse; his mouth hung open in astonishment. At last he was able to speak.

"My Lady, forgive me. To be here I have fought with terror and horror out of my worst night-mares, and yet within a day I meet beauty that exceeds my sweetest dreams. How can this be?"

The Lady laughed again, her sweet tinkling laugh. "Gemree, my lord, my destiny, help me from my horse; we will walk, and we will talk together."

Gemree leapt from Swiftsure's back and holding out his arms caught Tashka as she slid from Dark Star. She took his hand, and with half a skip that made her seem like a young impetuous child, she set off with Gemree along the river bank. Swiftsure and Dark Star stood patiently and contentedly pulling at the clumps of grass.

For the whole of that idyllic day they walked through meadows and along river banks. They sat and talked whilst they carelessly threw twigs into the gently flowing blue waters of the river. They laughingly blew the cotton headed seeds from the heads of the dandelions that grew around them. They were children, and they enjoyed children's pleasures. And yet, in that single day Gemree learned many things from The Lady of Mircrascar. He learned of the Three Worlds:

Highworld, which was the world of Arac, the world of the Synod Mountains and the Great Sea, the world of Boldeg and Hanlon, of Oblivia – and of course of Sodah, and the Prophecy that his destiny bade him fulfil; Trueworld, the world of the Waterfalls and the Plantmass, the world of the Cavern of the Bat and the Pit of Snakes, the World of The Lady of Micrascar; and Earthworld, a world from which would come The Thirteenth Knight. A world approached through the Gateway of Irenhold, the Gateway that he must open for The Follower. These Three Worlds, each occupying the same Space in the same Time and yet each unaware of the other. Lost in a dimensional fold where time and space are the same and at the same time different. Where, people, places and things, geography and history overlap each other and yet remain apart.

He tried hard to understand how he could be sitting by the banks of a river in Trueworld with the most beautiful maiden in a thousand worlds; and yet somehow, at the same time, in a different dimension this same space was probably occupied by another, and instead of a river there might be mountain or a forest. As he had wrestled with the hugeness of this concept The Lady of Micrascar had laughed and lightly touched his arm. "Gemree," she had said, "you are a brave Knight and you need not torment yourself with the miracles of the Three Worlds. Let me tell you now of the Great Knight of Rantoc."

So he had smiled and laid back in the willowing

grass. He had learned of a village in the far south of Trueworld.

A village called Rantoc. He had learned of the castle that dominated the river and the surrounding country. He had learned of an evil man, the Great Knight of Rantoc, who dominated the people of that unhappy land.

As the light of the idyllic day began to fade the Lady again laid her hand upon Gemree's arm. "My Lord" she said softly "It is time for you to go. Tomorrow you must prepare the way over the Pit of Snakes for The Follower. Swiftsure will help you in your task"

"When do we meet again my Lady?" asked Gemree.

She smiled, "First you had to cross the Plantmass, then you had to defeat the Great Bat and survive the Pit of Snakes.

These ordeals were written in the Prophecy, our meeting could only follow them. Soon you will meet the Great Knight of Rantoc in a battle that only one of you can survive. I pray my Lord that you and I will meet again before the Great Gates to Earthworld. On that day our time will be long and unhurried and I will tell you more of the Prophecy of the Trueworld. A Prophecy linked to your own, as night is linked to day." She paused, "I know, my Lord, how the Prophecy is written. I know the price for success, and I know the price of failure. I know that my destiny is to guide you if you succeed. Whether you succeed or fail is hidden from me." She rose to her feet and Gemree rose with her. The two fine horses had followed them through that long day, walking when they walked, resting when they rested. They now grazed quietly close by.

"Swiftsure – come!" The command from the Lady was almost a whisper, but the horse pricked its ears and walked silently over to nuzzle the Lady's hand. Gemree took hold of the white mane and swung himself up into the saddle.

"Goodbye my Lord, I pray we will meet again soon."

"Goodbye my Lady," he smiled," there is no power in the three worlds strong enough to prevent it."

The Lady of Micrascar turned, and without looking back began to walk towards the distant forest. Unbidden, the great black horse followed. The sun awoke Gemree the following day and he sat up to see Swiftsure grazing patiently nearby. The finished aqueduct lay on the river bank. He had no memory of the ride back to this place; it was of no importance. He inspected the aqueduct and noted with satisfaction that the sun had done its work. The mud had dried bone hard on the frame work of reeds and bullrushes and a million small cracks crazed its surface. He was pleased with his handiwork. Taking the remaining length of cornstalk rope he fashioned a simple loop in one end and secured the other end to the aqueduct. Passing the loop over Swiftsure's head he then led the animal into the water, pulling the structure behind him. Once in the water, and whilst still in the shallows, Gemree splashed the inside of the aqueduct and worked the crazed surface of the mud until it shone with a smooth wetness. When he was happy with his work he pulled himself back onto the river's bank and collecting an armful of slow burning torches he had made, he put them in the bottom of the aqueduct. Making his way to the horse's head he was now ready to brave the inner mountain and the Pit of Snakes once more, and taking hold of the cornstalk loop and kicking with his feet he began to swim towards the opposite bank leading the animal as he did so. The aqueduct floated easily and, it was not too long before the strength of the fine animal had overcome the steep slope leading from the river to the entrance of the mountain's cavern. Soon Swiftsure, Gemree and the remarkable aqueduct had started their journey back down the swift flowing stream.

With his strong muscles it was a surprisingly easy journey back to the Pit of Snakes. Fixing the bulrush torches around the walls to give light, and with Swiftsure's help, he eventually manoeuvred the aqueduct into position across the pit and firmly anchored the two ends. He watched with great satisfaction as the water, which had been plunging over the precipice into the pit below, willingly altered its course to run tumbling through the narrow channel and rejoin the stream that it had parted company with eons ago. He smiled with satisfaction in the knowledge that nothing now would hinder the passage of The Follower.

Taking just one more look at the water, now flowing swiftly through the clever box section of his making, he knew that The Follower could now complete his journey to the sun-kissed meadows of Trueworld without let or hindrance.

Taking Swiftsure by the rope that still hung around his neck he headed back down the stream. Towards daylight. Towards warmth. And ultimately, he knew, towards the radiance of the Lady of Micrascar.

Chapter 14

The Great Knight of Rantoc

Shores of the utmost west,
You who have waited long
Follow the trumpets quest
Break forth its swelling song

The Mountains of Sodah were bleak and austere, and yet they gave up a secret that led to a land of lush green forests, golden meadows and blue rivers. Like amoeba the masses on the hillsides separated and reformed, like columns of marching ants creating their colonies.

Like a black thread they wound around the mountain's face to disappear into a cleft – no wider than a man and a horse. Guns were shouldered, cannons were dismantled, swords sheathed as man upon endless man, slid into the very flesh of the mighty mountain range, on a journey to its heart – and beyond.

A journey which would spell the death and destruction of the fair land of Arac.

For several days Gemree had ridden alongside the river. After his return from the Pit he had spent two idle days in the Meadow of Micrascar hoping that the Lady would come back to him, although, in his heart he knew that it must be as she had said. He must meet and defeat the Great Knight of Rantoc in battle and secure the way for The Follower. The way to the Great Gateway. He WOULD see his Lady again. He would see her in that nomansland between courage and sacrifice, between life hard won, and death willingly given. That is where he would spend a last few precious hours, and that prize was all that he needed to spur him on to his next ordeal. He did not understand how the elements of the Prophesy fitted together, but he knew that, understanding or not he would make that last willing sacrifice. But oh, to understand …

His mind juggled the jigsaw pieces. He could feel the boundaries of the Good and of the Evil. He could see the shape of the tangible and of the intangible. For good there was King Synod and King Pylon. His dear brothers, the Knights of Arac. The twelve squires, including his own brave and loyal Pimm. And Taskha, his Lady, The Lady of Micrascar. So much in the name of Good. For Evil, and still he shuddered at the memories, the hideous creature of the Cavern. The writhing Snakes in the Pit, and the as yet unmet, Great Knight of Rantoc. There was the tangible: the Waterfalls and the Plantmass, The Saddlestone, and the Great Gates of Slaco. There was the intangible: the Visions and the Dream, the Ordeals and the Sacrifice. Then there was the unknown: the Tokens, The Follower, and the Thirteenth

Knight. There were the three worlds: Highworld, Trueworld and Earthworld.

"My mind," thought Gemree, "will explode with such questions." And then he saw it.

It had been hidden by the trees that stood tall in the loop of the rivers bend. Now it towered before him, black and forbidding. Four round, battlement-topped turrets pierced the sky. Thick stone walls rose out of the river itself. But that was not all. At first glance it appeared to Gemree that the river and the castle moulded together, as did the surrounding countryside, both meadow and wood. For long moments he stared, unable to understand how the whole countryside seemed to have been absorbed into this sinister and dominating structure. Gradually the picture became clear. The castle was built on a slight rise in the ground where the river looped around and almost doubled back on itself. The effect was that although Gemree was riding along the river's bank, the castle was now exactly opposite him. The river continued to flow, no longer to Gemree's right hand, but to his left. The river itself formed a natural moat to the front of the castle. It had been tapped to flow in a circle from the right-hand turret, around the rear of the castle, to rejoin the river by the left-hand tower. Between these two tall turrets was a huge iron portcullis. It was approached by a drawbridge that spanned the river, from the bank upon which he now stood, to the very threshold of two massive oaken doors. Each was higher than a house and gave access to the castle beyond. On the bend of the river, about two hundred paces from the drawbridge, was a man-made weir. The waters crashed over this obstacle in a tumbling fury, to the river's new level some dozen feet below. From that point they flung themselves with white-crested tops, under the drawbridge.

What hung below the drawbridge made Gemree recoil with horror. From the topmost plank to a point well below the river's surface, was the cruellest tangle of iron spikes that it could be possible to imagine. Worse than that, from constant immersion in the bubbling water the ironworks had become thick and red with rust. A rust that coloured the water like blood flecked foam. The reason for this inhuman barrier was clear. Any small boat that rounded the river's bend, unaware of a hazard ahead, would be tossed to its destruction. It was clear that there was no way past the castle by river, be it day or night. So, what of the land? Nature had done much of the work that made the Castle invulnerable: the bend of the river, the thickness of the forest. These formed natural defences that left little for man to add to. Someone, presumably under the direction of the Great Knight, had taken care of the rest.

The river looped in a great pear shape. A tall tangle of trees ran to the very neck of that pear. This left some 400 yards of open ground from the river bank on which Gemree stood, to where it completed its loop directly opposite. The drawbridge reached the bank some 200 yards away. From the drawbridge to a point where the trees grew thick, a fortified stone wall had been built, not high, but impassable. Close to the drawbridge was a huge arched opening with gates that folded back into the dark spaces behind. In this opening, seated on a horse that made Swiftsure look like a pony, was the mightiest warrior that Gemree had ever seen. He guessed that the height of the wall was probably a little above the height of two men. The great arched opening came to within a foot or two of the top, and yet this Knight, on his huge black horse, had had to dip his head as he rode beneath its portals. He sat silently, a formidable sight. His armour, as black as the horse's coat, was without device. The massive saddle bore a great ornate pommel and rested upon gold embroidered companions. A magnificent armoured head-piece with a great black plume completed the awesome sight. The Knight sat with his arms held loosely by his side. One hand held a mighty battle axe. The other, his left, grasped a broadsword that most men would need two hands to wield, but which, in his great fist looked like little more than a large hunting knife. His chest was broad and heavy and the muscles bulged even through the fine chainmail of his black armour. He controlled his great horse without effort, and when he spoke his voice made the world silent.

"My Lord Gemree, I have been waiting." Gemree pulled himself upright on Swiftsure and with the slightest pressure of his knees, he turned to face the man. He continued to speak.

"You are not welcome at the Castle of Rantoc. No-one is welcome at the Castle of Rantoc.

This field will be your journey's end as it has been the end of so many other journeys.

There is no destination beyond Rantoc."

Gemree spoke, "I am the Prince Gemree, Twelfth Knight of Arac of the Highworld" he paused and smiled "I have reached my destination. My mission is to destroy its Great Knight.

A huge laugh broke from Rantoc. "I have heard stories of Arac. It has been written that one day one of that little world's heroes would come to destroy me. I have waited eagerly to do battle with one who would pretend to be my match, one who would pretend to share my skill at arms, and yet, I must confess to a great feeling of disappointment. What do I see? I do not see a hero warrior cut in the mould of the mighty; I see a mere boy. A boy without muscle or girth," he paused before he continued. "And yet," he mused, "I see you ride Swiftsure, the horse that with its brother, Dark Star, was mine before I was cheated from both by the Lady of Micrascar. So Gemree, I wonder, do you have some talent that is not immediately apparent to me? Whether you have such skill or not, is nothing to me, for worthy adversary or not, your killing will be a pleasure." With these words the Great Knight wheeled his great horse, and ducking his head rode back under the stone portal. The great gates clanged shut behind him and Gemree watched as he galloped across the drawbridge and into the castle.

All that day Gemree sat quietly on Swiftsure waiting for Rantoc to re-appear, but the great gates remained firmly closed. He allowed himself to reflect on his inevitable battle with the Great Knight. He studied his battleground. As he had already noted, the curving river formed his boundary to his right and the thick forest to his left. The distance between the two was barely 200 yards. Behind him the river, once around the bend stretched back straight and true all the way to the Meadows of Micrascar. His mind registered this retreat, if retreat was needed. Ahead, and halfway across the field, stretching from the drawbridge to the forest, was the thick battlement wall with its great gates. This wall was some 200 yards in front of him and so their battle field would be some 200 yards by 200 yards with impenetrable boundaries to right and left. Rantoc would always have a limited retreat back through his oaken gates.

Gemree noticed that along the wall stood an untidy row of random stone slabs, tombstones carelessly stuck in the ground. There was still no sign of the Great Knight and giving Swiftsure his head, he trotted over to the wall. Strangely enough, all the stones, and there were over twenty of them, bore nothing but a date, a date meaningless to Gemree who had no knowledge of the marking of time in the Trueworld. He was about to turn away when he was struck by the last stone in the line. Whereas the others were old and weathered, this one stood straight and shone with newness. He rode up to it, and what he saw caused him to rock back in amazement. On the stone, newly cut and engraved in gold was a simple inscription.

THE LORD GEMREE
Killed here in Battle
on the Day of the Eighteenth Moon
7431

As he read these words the air was filled with that great booming laugh that would make the birds stop singing if birds inhabited this accursed place. He realised that the first blow in the battle, the battle of wits, had been struck and that all the glory had gone to the Great Knight. Without a word he turned Swiftsure's head and galloped furiously across the field and around the river's bend. Once out of sight of the castle he pulled the horse to a halt. Dismounting, he made camp for the night, cursing himself for being a fool and reacting to his shock just as Rantoc would have wished. He realised that part of the Great Knight's strategy was to mentally unnerve him, and was determined that, not only would that strategy fail, but that he would win the battle of wit and wills. When he had settled Swiftsure, he sat cross-legged on the ground and, closing his eyes, allowed his mind to float back to Arac, to the dream of Synod. With his help he would summon up the will and the courage to win this unknightly battle. Long before he slept, he knew exactly what he must do.

The next morning, as the sun crept over the rim of the horizon to herald the dawn, it fell upon Gemree. He sat, ramrod straight, upon Swiftsure on the edge of the field of Rantoc, facing the great gates. His armour shone as the early sun's rays fell upon it. From dawn on that first day until the sun sank over the opposite horizon to bring the dusk he sat, unmoving. He took no water, he took no food, and, his eyes never left those great oaken gates through which Rantoc would come. Not until the darkness was well established, did he turn back to camp, to water, to food and to rest. During the previous long night's meditation he had drawn great strength from Synod, and now he knew, not hoped, but knew, that he could and would win this battle of nerve against Rantoc. He visualised the knight, pacing the castle, his eyes involuntarily drawn with greater and greater frequency to the slit windows. Windows from where he could see his adversary, a Knight of whom he knew nothing, save that he had travelled from another world to defeat him in battle. Rantoc, unlike Gemree, had nowhere to go. Eventually he would have to come out to fight, and Gemree knew that each watching day would increase his advantage and unsettle Rantoc the more. After he had settled Swiftsure and satisfied his own hunger and thirst, he once more fell into his cross-legged position of meditation. Another night passed.

From the sun's rise until its setting on four days more Gemree sat unmoving on the field of Rantoc. From the gathering of dusk until the breaking of dawn for four more nights Gemree drew his strength from Synod and from his meditation. Surprisingly he felt no tiredness. As the dawn broke on the fifth morning, the oaken gates were thrown back with an almighty crash. With a bellow that turned even that sound into insignificance, the Great Knight of Rantoc appeared. He held his great war axe in one hand, and his mighty sword in the other. He called loudly to Gemree across the intervening distance.

"Well, brave Knight, you have read your epitaph, now prepare for its fulfilment.

With a loud bellow the Great Knight of Rantoc spurred his horse into a gallop, one hand whirling the huge war axe above his head, while the other held the impressive two-handed broadsword aloft. Despite the terrifying sight of this great horse and magnificently splendid Knight bearing down upon him at great speed, Gemree made no attempt to suppress the smile that came to his lips or the laughter that bubbled over in his heart. The Great Knight was angry. Gemree had won the psychcological war. As he, and every Knight trained for combat knew, anger was a poor companion to sit beside you on the field of battle.

THE GREAT KNIGHT OF RANTOC

Anger dulled your vision and slowed your thinking. Anger made your limbs act without asking permission of your brain. Such was the case now. The sun hung low in the morning sky, but already it shone brightly. This morning, as every morning it had risen directly behind Gemree's back as he sat impassively on Swiftsure facing the oaken gates. A Knight who was battle tuned, would have circled the field of battle to ensure that the sun, if not giving him favour, was at worst neutralised. In his anger, Rantoc had no thought beyond humiliating his opponent. He charged unthinkingly towards Gemree who knew that whilst he could see his every movement clearly, for Rantoc, he would be no more than a blurred shape in front of a bright circle of light. Keeping the sun directly to his back he began to canter towards the charging Knight, who was now bearing down on him at full gallop. He manoeuvred himself so that Rantoc would pass him by on his left side. Thus he would expose himself to a blow from his own right sword arm, whilst having to make his own blow, not with the madly whirling axe, where a lucky strike could bring a premature end to the proceedings, but with the heavy and cumbersome broadsword wielded in his left hand. His blow would be at a target that was not only blurred by the sun, but which, by his movement, would require that it be made across, both his own body, and that of his horse. Rantoc did not falter in his gallop and slashed harmlessly with his broadsword, a blow that passed several inches above Gemree's head.

Gemree had reigned in Swiftsure, so that he was now almost standing still. With unerring accuracy, and using a trick taught to him by his old and clever Knightmaster when he was but a boy, he struck. Not at the man whom he knew could, under his tough chain mail withstand many blows. Nor at the horse, but at the girths beneath the horse's belly that held in place the huge and ornate saddle. Despite the horse's speed the blows accuracy was uncanny and without drawing even the merest spot of blood from the horse's flesh, the saddles straps parted. As the horse continued its gallop unchecked, Gemree wheeled around to watch the helpless gyrations of the Great Knight, as, with arms waving helplessly, he strove in vain to prevent the inevitable. It was hopeless, and as the magnificent saddle slipped beneath the horse's belly, Knight, broadsword and axe hit the ground with a thunderous crash. A crash that would have put an end to the battle with any lesser man. Not so the Great Knight. For some long moments he lay there, still and winded, the breath knocked out of his body, his left arm bent unnaturally beneath him. His horse had galloped on almost to the fringe of the trees, and now stood unconcerned as it pulled at clumps of grass with its teeth. Rantoc struggled to his feet. The horse's ears pricked as he gave a piercing whistle and a bellow, that left Gemree in no doubt that his anger had in no way diminished. As the horse trotted back to his stranded master Gemree knew that he had a choice. He could take the battle to Rantoc before he had the chance to remount,or he could bide his time and rely on his horsemanship,which already he believed was superior, to improve the odds in his favour. He knew that hand to hand he would have little chance against this huge man without his strength first being seriously weakened. If he succeeded in pulling him off his horse the battle would be as good as over. No, he had already made his decisions during those long nights of meditation. He would use his greater fitness and agility, and he believed his greater wit against the indisputably superior strength of Rantoc. He would wear the Knight down degree by slow degree, and most of all, he would ensure that at no stage did he let go of the great anger that would ultimately consume him.

Gemree once more turned the horse's head and cantered towards the oaken gates. He wheeled around and quietly watched as Rantoc cut free the hanging saddle and then picked up his broadsword in his right hand. Deftly, he leapt back onto the, now saddleless back of his great stallion. Gemree noted with some satisfaction that the war axe still lay on the ground where it had fallen, and Rantoc's left arm hung limply by his side. It was time for him to turn the knife and inflame Rantoc's anger still further. He spoke. "Sir Rantoc the unhorsed," he called loudly across the field, "thank you sir for such an amusing show, but, if it's all the same to you, may we continue the battle?" With the now familiar bellow Rantoc spurred his horse forward and within just a few yards had reached full gallop. This time the sun was at his back and shining in Gemree's eyes.

Gemree sat there quite unconcerned, even though he had to screw up his eyes to keep Rantoc in proper focus. He waited a moment more and then began to canter towards the charging Knight. He did no want to stray too far from the Gates, but at the same time he needed to be far enough from them to encourage Rantoc not to slacken his breakneck gallop. The sun was now shining brightly in Gemree's eyes, but unlike Rantoc, he believed that he had the wit to turn it to his advantage. At a point about 50 yards out from the wall he reigned in and prepared to meet the swishing blade of Rantoc. He had to admire the brilliant horsemanship of the Knight, as, riding bareback and gripping and controlling the horse only with his powerful legs, he came on at frightening speed. Gemree held his own broadsword lightly with his left hand on the hilt and sat there looking confidently into the now dazzling sun. When Rantoc was no more than a dozen yards away, he brought his broadsword up to his waist. Grabbing the point in his right hand he positioned the flat, wide, and mirror bright blade so that the sun reflected off its surface. He directed the dazzling brightness, not at the man, but straight into the eyes of the charging horse. This sudden and blinding burst of light so alarmed the animal that it reared high on to its hind legs, pawing the air with its hooves. Even Rantoc's superb horsemanship could not prevent him sliding down the animal's back and once more crashing upon the hard ground.

This time Gemree seized the horse's reigns while it was still disorientated by the blinding light. Quickly he led it at a fast canter to the far edge of the field where he deftly tethered it. He then turned and galloped back through the open oak gates. Once safely on the other side he dismounted, closed the gates and slid the great wooden locking bar in place. He sprinted up the flight of stone steps that led to the battlements. Standing with his feet firmly apart he looked down on the scene below. This time it took Rantoc much longer to rise to his feet, and when he did so it was to look upon an empty field. As he turned around, he saw his horse well out of reach, firmly tethered and quietly pulling at the low branches of the tree that held him. Rantoc gave his whistled command and the animal made a half-hearted effort to respond, but held firmly by the tree, he soon gave up and became pre-occupied with his meal. Rantoc picked up his sword in his right hand, his left arm still hung helplessly by his side. In the middle of the field lay his discarded war axe and the ornate saddle. He began to walk towards them but was stilled by Gemree's voice from behind him singing tunefully.

"The Lord Rantoc, a bold knight of course,
Has to walk for he fell off his horse.
His foe must pay an awful price,
He fell from his horse, not once but twice"

With a great roar Rantoc rushed to the gate in a stumbling run. "Open these gates and fight like a Knight" he bellowed, don't run like a coward."

Gemree beamed down at him, "Why my Lord, you must calm yourself. Now please, rest your poor old bones, heaven knows they have been through a lot already today, and the sun has barely run a quarter of its course."

"Let me in, you cannot hide from me!" Bellowed Rantoc,

"Hide? Now do I look as if I am hiding?" said Gemree in a most reasonable tone. "No, not a bit of it. Now my Lord Rantoc, you just rest and get your breath back, and I will let you in, in due course." With this Gemree jumped off the battlements and ran back down the stone steps into the courtyard. He ignored the loud banging of Rantoc's sword hilt on the great door. He ignored the taunts of *Coward* that came from the anger filled Knight. The battle was too important for him to give way to foolish taunts. He was determined to think out every detail of the forthcoming battle, and to know his ground as well as did Rantoc himself.

He surveyed the scene. To his left there was the broad flight of stone steps that he had just ascended to get to the battlements. As he looked along the wall he noted that there were similar flights at regular intervals. The battlements themselves were high and narrow with barely room for two men to pass. The outer edge was formed by the great stone turrets that were designed to protect men from arrows or other missiles fired from outside the wall.

The inner edge was unguarded and a careless step would result in a tumble to the ground some 12 feet below. Along the length of the wall, evenly spaced, were four tall timber watch towers, each standing on three wooden tripod legs going right down to the base of the wall. Gemree sprinted back up the stone steps to the battlement to examine one of these towers. He found that it contained three large water barrels, a variety of hand missiles such as small rocks and misshapen pieces of iron. Also within the tower there were a large timber chests that, although firmly locked gave easily to Gemree's sword, to reveal a selection of hand weaponry; knives, small swords and suchlike.

The height of the towers exceeded that of the battlements by some ten to twelve feet and were approached by a rough wooden ladder. The towers stood away from the battlements by some six or seven feet. From the roof of the tower hung a large brass bell. The bell rope dangled right down to the courtyard below so that it could be rung without climbing the tower.

He eyed all of this with great satisfaction and was almost ready to put his plan into action.

Like all good plans his was simple. He knew that he had the skill to defeat Rantoc. After all, was he not the most skilful of all the Knights of Arac with sword and lance? However, he did recognise Rantoc's great strength, and realized that he must tire the mighty warrior to the point of exhaustion if he was not to be beaten into submission by sheer power alone. He had seen two major weaknesses in his adversary. That of arrogance, and that of anger. He intended to play upon those two weaknesses. He knew that as long as he kept the anger at fever pitch then Rantoc would only allow his body, and not his mind, to fight the battle. In his arrogance he would believe it unthinkable that a warrior as great and as mighty as he could be beaten by one so young and, by comparison, so frail.

Gemree took the thick bell rope in his hand and began to pull on it until he had the great bell ringing loudly and with such momentum that it continued even after he had let go of the rope. He then ran along the battlement, and set each bell ringing, sending out a deafening message of defiance to the Knight who still bellowed, and banged his sword on the doors below. It was now time to further fuel the anger that now all but consumed him. He jumped up again on the battlements and looked down.

"Rantoc, do you hear the bells, they are to warn the world that there is a madman locked out of his own castle. A madman who has twice been unhorsed without his adversary offering a blow in anger. Indeed Rantoc, they will sing songs of this day," Gemree threw back his head and laughed loudly. He watched with satisfaction as the Knight, all rational thought deserting him, threw himself repeatedly against the thick and unyielding doors. Gemree drew back. "I think," he said quietly to himself, "it is time to do battle with a madman." He ran lightly down the steps and placed his face against the door, listening to the thumps as Rantoc hurled himself, senselessly, against the three-inch oak. Timing his actions to perfection, he quietly lifted the locking bar as he heard Rantoc withdraw for another assault against the door. He hit the door with a great crash. With nothing to restrain it, it flew open and deposited Rantoc, for the third time, a bundle of arms and legs, upon the hard ground.

Gemree stood there with feet apart and his hands upon his hips – "Well, my Lord, it seems that you spend more time on your back than you do on your feet, shall we fight before you fall yet again?" Rantoc raised himself on to one knee and reached for the hilt of his broadsword.

"You will pay dearly for the insults that you have heaped upon me today," he snarled, and as he did so he stood, sweeping his broadsword upwards in a single motion of great power and devastating accuracy. A blow that so easily could have been fatal. But Gemree was ready. At the peak of his fitness, and skilful beyond all others in Arac, he parried the blow easily, although he inwardly winced at the great power in which it was delivered. He made no attempt to counter the blow, the time was not yet right for hand to hand combat. Instead he turned and ran swiftly up the stone steps, knowing that Rantoc would follow him. Roaring like a stuck boar he did so, but Gemree had reached the top and turned before he was even half way. He looked up and shock registered on his face as he saw Gemree smiling broadly, and in the act of hurling one of the heavy water barrels down the stairs. He looked around but there was no escape; the barrel struck him firmly below the knees and knocked his legs from under him. The barrel burst and water cascaded over him. Although he had fallen, he had managed to maintain his grip on the steps and had not been knocked backwards. He pulled himself to his knees, and that was when the second barrel hit him, then the third. He reached the courtyard in an untidy collection of arms and legs, wetter than if he had swum the moat, and covered in the smashed remains of his own water barrels.

Keeping up the pressure Gemree ran back down the steps and standing on the lower flight looked down on the once more horizontal Knight. "Sir Knight, pray tell me how can we enjoy our friendly tussle when you keep taking time out to rest in this way. Perhaps it is your age. Would you like to rest and have us continue tomorrow?" For once he overestimated his own abilities, and underestimated Rantoc's. In a movement that was little more than a blur, the

Knight shot out his legs and closed them like scissors one behind and one in front of Gemree's knees. In that one twisting movement Gemree was brought to the ground. Instinctively he rolled as he fell. It is as well that he did, for the great broadsword struck the ground with frightening force exactly where his head had been just seconds before. This strike was just a part of one movement that brought the Knight to his feet. Gemree was now lying full length on the ground and Rantoc towered over him like a giant. Gemree's sword was still in its sheath, but he was able to pull it clear just in time to cover his head as the next blow fell upon him. The power was so great that his sword was driven back towards his face by fully eighteen inches. He realized that once more he had come within a hair's breadth of death. As Rantoc raised his sword again he was able to roll over and rise to one knee. From this position he was more competently able to stop the next crushing blow. Then he was on his feet, vowing never to be complacent again, and never to underestimate this man they called the Great Knight of Rantoc.

Given space, he was able to move away and gradually mount the steps to the battlements. Rantoc followed him. The battle was now on. He moved quickly for a big man, and the recent hand to hand confrontation, where he had so obviously been the stronger, had served to release, and to reduce, much of the anger that had been in him. He was beginning to think like a Knight; Gemree knew that this, coupled with his strength and skill could be a fatal combination. A mighty blow from his sword bit into the stone step where his feet had been just moments before. Gemree had the temporary advantage of height however, and was able to rain a number of accurate blows, though easily parried, upon the head and shoulders of Rantoc. Seeing no advantage in this exchange Gemree turned and bounded up the remaining steps encouraging Rantoc to do the same. The big knight was already markedly slower than Gemree, who, having reached the battlements had ample time to put the next part of his plan into action.

Quickly he climbed into the first of the watch towers and dislodged the ladder so that it fell into the courtyard below. Rantoc drew level with the tower, and looking up brandished his sword at Gemree. "Sir," he shouted, "what kind of Knight are you who shrinks from combat? You shame the colours that you wear. You shame the sacred sign of Arac upon your chest. But, most of all you shame the brotherhood of Knights of which you are a member." Gemree did not answer, instead he removed his plumed helmet and let his long blonde hair fall free over his shoulders. Rantoc saw what he had long suspected. Gemree was little more than a boy, perhaps 17 or 18 years old. He was as slim as a girl and his eyes sparkled, a bright clear blue, a colour that so often goes with, and complements blonde hair. Gemree laughed. "I am no coward Rantoc, and the only one who has been shamed this day is The Great

Knight of Rantoc. The Great Knight of whom songs will surely be written."

Gemree began to sing in a soft tuneful voice.

"On his horse the Knight of Rantoc sat,
The sun came up and shone into his eyes
He bellowed as he charged the Knight of Arac,
His girth is cut, now on the ground he lies,
His girth is cut, now on the ground he lies.
But brave he is, he mounts and bareback rides
To smite this shameful youth – oh damn his eyes!
But oh, he's blinded by that sun again,
He falls, once more upon the ground he lies.
He falls, once more upon the ground he lies."

Gemree's youthful voice rang out, each word as clear as crystal. Rantoc let out his now familiar bellow.

"That song will never be sung boy, rather the song that tells of the death of an upstart boy who thought he was a Knight. Now I see you trapped in my own watch tower. Your end will not be long coming."

Great Rantoc rushed the stony steps, at worst
This piffling youth he will be cut to size,
But down roll water barrels and burst;
Once more upon the ground Great Rantoc lies!
Once more upon the ground Great Rantoc lies!"

With a roar Rantoc rushed to the next watch tower and struggled with the ladder, intending to use it to reach Gemree. The young man watched, and waited patiently until the ladder had been leant against the tower that Gemree occupied. As Rantoc began to climb upwards, Gemree jumped up on the tower's parapet and taunted Rantoc yet again.

"Once more upon the ground Great Rantoc lies!
Once more upon the ground Great Rantoc lies."

Everything was going exactly to plan. He waited until Rantoc leapt into the tower, and then, grabbing the bell rope, swung himself off the parapet into mid air. Choosing his time he let go of the rope and landed safely back on the battlements 12 feet below. He turned and quickly pulled the ladder free so that it went crashing into the courtyard below.

Letting go of the bell rope he allowed it to swing harmlessly beneath the tower. Rantoc could swing on it as Gemree had done, but his course would lead him on to the point of Gemree's sword. He was, for all practical purposes, a prisoner in his own watch tower, just as Gemree had intended.

He smiled broadly, and a little vainly, at his cleverness. The veins stood out like thick ropes in Rantoc's neck, his face was red with fury as he realized how he had been tricked.

"Well Rantoc," said Gemree, "It appears that I have outwitted you as the Prophecy said I would. Regrettably that is not enough. My destiny requires that I defeat you.

Not only must we fight, but we must fight and I must win. You have shown yourself to be a man with abundant brawn, but pitifully little brain. I am no coward, but my mission is too important for me to allow you to best me. Look below." Rantoc moved to the edge of the parapet and looked down; what he saw made him recoil with shock. Piled high around the wooden legs of the tower were heaped bundles of tinder dry brushwood. He looked back at the young Knight and saw him remove his tinder box from his tunic and, making a spark, set fire to one of the many torches that hung along the battlement wall. He watched in horror as Gemree waited until it was flaming brightly, and then calmly dropped it on to the brushwood pile. In moments, deep orange flame was leaping up around the watch tower legs. In no time at all the fire was burning fiercely.

"My Lord Rantoc," said Gemree, "you have a choice."

"You can swing on the bell rope and meet your end on the point of my sword, or you can wait but a moment or two to be engulfed in flame and pitched into the fire that is now raging below."

Rantoc's choice was one that again took Gemree completely by surprise at the speed of its execution and the bravery of the act. While

Gemree was still speaking Rantoc put one foot on the parapet and launched himself into space, heading straight for Gemree over 12 feet below. As he watched this huge shape hurtling towards him Gemree hurriedly tried to unsheathe his sword, cursing himself for the third time for underestimating this great warrior. The sword was only half way out of its sheath when the full weight of Rantoc struck Gemree squarely and sent him flying back against the buttressed battlements. He hit the wall with such a force that the breath was knocked from his body. He lay on the ground, panting, in an effort to pull himself together. It was fortunate for Gemree that Rantoc had not landed on top of him, for if he had the battle could well have been all over. As it happened, The Great Knight himself had landed heavily, but non-the-less had escaped certain defeat by his quick wittedness and courage. The two Knights slowly stood up to face one another, and, for the first time they faced each other on equal terms. Now that Gemree had got his breath back he was feeling fit and strong. Rantoc, on the other hand, had clearly landed very badly and winced as he placed his weight on his right leg. The combined effects of the falls from the horse, the fall down the stone stairs, and this last massive and ungainly leap from the watch tower had taken their toll. He now moved cautiously, and obviously with some pain and discomfort. Nevertheless he was still a Knight with great experience, and, as they faced each other

THE GREAT KNIGHT OF RANTOC

Gemree knew that he would still need every ounce of his own courage and skill to come out of this combat the victor. Yet the victor he must be. Not just for his own sake, but for the sake of the Prophecy, The Follower, and for his King.

Rantoc was still on one knee and in the act of pushing himself upwards when, with great agility, Gemree struck the first blow. A fierce, two handed, downward strike aimed at the vulnerable part of the neck where the chain mail jerkin met the balaclava type headpiece. Rantoc parried the blow with ease and the three swiftly delivered blows that followed it. Gemree, knew that his advantage had been lost, and retreated, jumping on to the battlement wall. From his lower position on the walkway, Rantoc could only aim slashing blows at Gemree's legs, blows which the agile young Knight avoided with ease. Gemree, on the other hand, was able to rain two-handed blows down upon the Knight's head and shoulders. There was a danger to this course of which he was well aware. While he was unlikely to receive a mortal blow, it was possible that Rantoc could dislodge him from his perch and send him tumbling into the river below, from where he would be swept on to that cruel tangle of spikes below the drawbridge. He took a moment to look up into the sky. The sun was now almost overhead, and he realized that this curious battle had been raging for half the day. Although Rantoc was the most affected by the battle, with his left arm hanging helplessly by his side, and his right leg dragging noticeably as he walked neither man had any wound that could be considered serious – certainly not mortal. Single mindedly, Gemree reverted to his original plan of heaping insult and humiliation upon the Great Knight in an effort to stoke his anger to mistake making fever pitch. Ignoring the taunts of "coward" he began to move swiftly along the battlement causing Rantoc to break into a shuffling run to keep up. When he had reached the stone steps, he jumped down and ran lightly into the courtyard. There he waited. By the time Rantoc reached the last step he was panting heavily. Gemree judged that he could safely indulge in some serious and strength-sapping hand to hand fighting. Matching his actions to his thoughts, he threw himself forward into a roll. Before Rantoc could appreciate what was happening, he had brought the flat of his broadsword violently against the back of Rantoc's knees. He completed his roll and came lightly to his feet, now behind Rantoc. To his great surprise the Great Knight found that Gemree's unorthodox move had resulted in him landing heavily on his knees as his legs collapsed beneath him. With a loud laugh Gemree placed his foot between Rantoc's shoulder blades, and, kicking forward sent the half balanced Knight pitching face down into the ground, still mud wet from the bursting water barrels.

Gemree made no attempt to press home his advantage. He knew that he did not have the strength of arm to drive the point of his sword through the strong chain mail armour. And, in any event, he had already decided how the fight must end, if the end was to be in his favour. The time had come to lift this combat from the realms of farce, and to place it in the domain of legend where it would remain for ever. Rantoc had dropped his sword as he had fell, and Gemree now stooped down and picked it up. Rantoc stood, towering above the boy who calmly waited, with his own sword hanging loosely in his right hand, and Rantoc's huge blade in his left. He had not replaced his helmet and his face looked younger that ever. He smiled broadly at the great towering figure in front of him. The wind lifted his long blonde hair from his shoulders and his eyes sparkled

"My Lord Rantoc," said Gemree, "our fight is not one of hatred. In truth, I know not why we fight, other than that the Prophecy wills that it must be so. I have seven ordeals to fulfil; only by succeeding at one, can I move on to the next. This is my sixth ordeal, the final one before my willing death. I sought to humiliate you, to insult you and to give you great anger. In so doing I have used such weapons as have been given to me, my youth, my agility and my wit. I could not hope to beat you by strength and courage alone, for you have proved that you have that in great abundance. The legend of The Great Knight Of Rantoc is known throughout Trueworld, this much I know. As a Knight, one of the rare brotherhood of Knights to which we all belong, I honour you now, with my sword, and pray that you will honour me with yours." With these words Gemree tossed the huge sword to Rantoc who caught it deftly.

"My Lord Gemree, you speak only of your destiny, but I too have a mission. For many years I have kept a lonely vigil at this place, I have challenged, and I have defeated, all who would pass. I know of your Prophecy, I know of The Follower who will tread the path that you must clear. I know that he must pass through the Gateway of Irenhold to Earthworld. It is Slaco, the keeper of the Gate, who placed me here. You are not just another battle, you are the battle for which I was created, and I cannot let you win. But, as you have shown me honour, so, by my sword will I honour you. He pointed the blade forward and Gemree did the same. The points touched and held together like a long lingering handshake. Withdrawing the blades each held their sword in front of their face with the blade pointing upwards.

"May your God fight by your side my Lord Rantoc," said Gemree.

"And may your God guide your arm," Rantoc replied. The giant warrior, and the slightly built boy began carefully to circle each other to see who could find the opening to strike the first blow.

What followed in that long afternoon was surely the stuff of legend. The sky which despite the bright sun had remained a dark purple grey since Gemree's arrival in Rantoc five days earlier, had suddenly brightened as if the gods themselves had at last approved the conflict. Rantoc showed little distress from his damaged left arm and bore down on Gemree with mighty strokes of his broadsword. Gemree knew that, had he been able to wield that blade with both hands, the fight would have been of short duration and he would never have been able to withstand the power of the assault. Rantoc's damaged right leg did however cause him greater difficulty, and Gemree was grateful for the decreased mobility, often resulting in the great flashing blade missing him by the slightest whisper. For his part, Gemree defended well, he had neither the strength nor the power to match Rantoc blow for blow, but his reflexes were honed to perfection and his agility was that of a cat. Using both hands to wield his sword it seemed that wherever Rantoc's blade fell, Gemree's was there to deflect it. So the fight went on, across the courtyard, up and along the battlements, and even on to the drawbridge itself. Always Rantoc the assailant, with his one handed blows and his shuffling forward step. Always forcing the pace, with Gemree being driven backwards, protecting himself from blow after devastating blow. The sun slowly began to set below the horizon, and dusk gathered the shadows together in every corner of the courtyard. From sunrise to sunset the battle had so far lasted, and since mid-day there had been no rest or respite for either combatant. It seemed that there could never be a victor, although had there been any witness to this struggle, all the odds would have rested with the Great Knight of Rantoc. Although he could not seem to penetrate Gemree's dogged defence, it seemed that every blow could be the last. It was clear that Gemree had not the strength to mount a counter attack that would cause distress to the mighty man. It was then, as darkness gradually overtook the final thin strands of day, that Rantoc made the mistake that nearly spelled disaster for them both.

They were fighting on the drawbridge. Rantoc had his back towards the battlement wall and had been driving Gemree closer and closer to the great iron portcullis that protected the entrance to the castle itself. Gemree had been forced onto his knees for the hundredth time and his arms were weary beyond description from the relentless battering that they and his sword had withstood. This time, as he glanced up into Rantoc's face he sensed a desperation in the Knight's manner that sent a chill through his whole body. It was then that Rantoc made the mistake. In an attempt to summon up every last ounce of power into the forthcoming blow, he stepped forward onto his right, and damaged leg, the leg that through all that long afternoon he had protected by dragging it behind him. To his weary mind, he could see that the end was in sight. He could see that just one more onslaught would be the last that Gemree would be able to absorb. As he crashed down onto his right foot with the sword high above his head, the damaged knee could not take his immense weight and collapsed under him causing him to stumble forward and fall directly onto the kneeling form of Gemree. Gemree had raised his sword parallel to his body to parry the expected blow and it was onto the flat of the blade that Rantoc fell. Whilst this did not cause him any serious injury, it caught him under the chin straight across the windpipe and had him gasping desperately for air. As he stumbled, he grabbed hold of Gemree, and although this halted his forward motion, it had the fatal result of deflecting him sideways, again onto his damaged leg. Gemree sized up the situation in an instant. Thrusting upwards from his knee, he grabbed Rantoc by the shoulder and twisted him violently sideways in an attempt to throw him over the side of the drawbridge and onto the tangle of rusty spikes below. The next thing he was aware of was cold and swirling water closing over his head. His move had been successful, but Rantoc, fighting to the end had firmly grabbed Gemree's sword arm thus ensuring that the two of them took this final plunge together. Except for the most outrageous piece of luck their final plunge it would have been.

The momentum of their fall had carried them a little way out from the drawbridge, and as they hit the water Gemree had felt the uncanny power of the current as it had picked them up and thrown them towards the spikes. He steeled himself for the impact that he knew would come. He felt the heart-stopping thump and heard the tearing of chain mail, and then of flesh. He felt no pain beyond the thousand bruises that already covered his slim body. He realized that he was still entwined with Rantoc, and then the truth hit him. It was Rantoc's chain mail, it was Rantoc's flesh that the spikes had torn into. In some miraculous, providential way, they had hit the water with Rantoc closest to the spikes. The current had not turned them but simply thrown them into the spikes in the positions in which they had hit the water. Rantoc had been Gemree's shield. Rantoc, had unwittingly given his life for Gemree.

With his lungs bursting he broke the surface of the river. With great difficulty he hauled himself up onto the drawbridge, and lying down where he flopped, he fell into a deep sleep. Every muscle, every sinew, every bone in his body cried out in pain. Gemree had fought his greatest battle, a battle that had started as the sun rose and ended as it set – and he had won. Dawn broke. The sun was bright and warm and the sky was the deepest blue. For the first time in Rantoc, birds sang. Gemree felt refreshed by his sleep, but still his body was racked with pain. On the drawbridge beside him lay his sword, the sword that had been his father's. He gave thanks that it had not tumbled into the river to be lost forever. He lay and looked over the edge of the

drawbridge. Beneath the surface he could see Rantoc's huge shape impaled firmly upon the rusty spikes, still in the death that he himself had prepared for The Follower.

Gemree had a great deal to do. The sun had risen and set three more times before he mounted Swiftsure and finally turned away from the field of Rantoc. It had been three days of intense activity. Thanks to the great strength of Swiftsure and the Great Knight's own horse, Rantoc's body had been removed from the spikes. The drawbridge had been dismantled and dragged to the middle of the field where, together with the great oaken gates, it had been burned in a huge fire that even now still smouldered. All that remained on that field of battle was a pile of twisted, metal spikes. The river now flowed an uninterrupted course, and the way past Rantoc was open to all.

Gemree's final act had been to bury The Great Knight below the tombstone that had once borne Gemree's name. A tombstone that now read:

> *"The Great Knight Of Rantoc"*
> *his Cause was wrong but*
> *he fought with Honour and with Courage*

Chapter 15

Tashka and the village

It was the most beautiful day that any world had ever seen. Gemree sat high on Swiftsure and looked down at the gently flowing waters of the river. Swans with long graceful necks glided effortlessly and elegantly across the surface. Busy brown and green ducks darted this way and that trailing the little fluffy bundles of their young behind them. Huge bright orange and green dragonflies flitted from bulrush to bulrush as they tried to fit a lifetime into their allotted 24 hours. On each side of the river multi-coloured meadows stretched forever. Above them song birds hovered, almost motionless, while the sun hung brightly in a cloudless sky. He was young. A young man with a destiny now seven parts fulfilled. He was riding a fine horse on a fine day, and soon he was to see his Lady Tashka, who made the most beautiful day appear ordinary, and the most ordinary, beautiful. Could this really be the same world that had revealed the Cavern of the Bat and the terror of the Pit of Snakes? Could it be the same world in which he had battled for a whole day against a powerful knight? The same world that had him leave that Knight dead below the benign river that now flowed gently at his feet, home to creatures of elegance and grace.

"My Lord Gemree, welcome." Gemree was jerked out of his day dreaming by the sound of the voice, so deeply and lovingly etched upon his memory. She stood before him a, vision of complete perfection. He dismounted, and patted Swiftsure's rump. The horse immediately cantered off to join Dark Star whom, untethered, grazed nearby. The Lady sat and smiled up at Gemree. He stood there drinking in the scene so that it would never leave his memory. She sat amongst a circle of yellow celandines, of white daisies and blue cornflowers. These colours, on their green and golden background, appeared to shift and change like the patterns of a kaleidoscope. It was an illusion caused partly by the gentle warm breeze that rustled the tops of the flowers and grasses, but more by the dozens of butterflies that settled and then rose only to settle again upon the individual gems of that wonderful living tapestry.

"Sit with me Gemree, and let us talk. Soon it will be time for us to make the final journey to The Gateway, and its keeper Slaco." Gemree fell on to his knees beside her, the joy of seeing her, of being with her again, driving all the recent black thoughts out of his mind.

"My Lady," he said "just one journey made with you is worth a thousand journeys made alone. Let us talk now, but let not our talk be of visions and dreams, of ordeals or sacrifices. Let it be of you and of me, of here and of now." And so it was. Eventually the day faded into a night which wrapped itself around them with a dark comfort. That night they talked much and slept little, savouring every precious moment, each in the company of the other. The probing fingers of the dawn found them, just as the fleeting strands of the previous day had left them, bound by a love that knew its time was short. When the sun was high in the sky Tashka stood slowly. "My Lord, our time together is not yet over, but we have far to go and we must leave now." Gemree rose to his feet, and wandering over to Swiftsure and Dark Star took their bridles and led them back to where the Lady was now stretching her arms to the sun. They mounted, and, without encouragement, Swiftsure and Dark Star turned and began to walk towards the distant hills which were silhouetted against the sun.

They rode together, hand in hand, through the day's beauty. They followed the twisting and turning river for many miles. They passed small villages with beautiful houses. People rushed to see The Lady of Micrascar and hailed with loud and grateful voices "The Price Gemree – Slayer of Rantoc." Tashka laughed. "The story of your great deeds travels even faster than we do my Lord." A group of small children rushed hither and thither and periodically one of them would hurl himself to the floor, saying. "I am The Great Rantoc, look how I roll on the Ground." She laughed again, "My Lord, I believe that we are watching a legend in the making." Gemree's face clouded.

"He was a brave Knight my Lady, I took no pleasure in his death, which, but for a quirk of fate could so easily have been mine."

Tashka sensed his mood. "Do not be troubled Gemree, Rantoc was brave because he was a trained Knight, but he was an arrogant man. He did not believe that there was any power in the Three Worlds that could defeat him, and in this he was nearly right. But, Gemree, you must understand that Rantoc, for all his courage in battle, was a wicked man with a black heart. He was a man who had terrorised the people for many long years." She paused, "look into the sky Gemree, what do you see?"

"Why nothing my Lady, it is as it was before," said Gemree gazing upwards.

"No my Lord, it is not as it was before. Now the sun shines. Now the sky is blue, birds hover and sing. These people," she waved her hand towards the villagers, "they have lived half a lifetime beneath the darkened skies brought upon them by the terror of Rantoc. These children," again she indicated the happy group rolling around on the ground, "have never seen a bird flying above them, or heard its song."

Gemree remembered the dark purple of the sky as he had first come upon The Castle of Rantoc. Tashka continued. "You are their hero, it is you who have made their sun shine, do not belittle your actions, for you have slain an unbeatable monster. As you ride among them now, you are nothing less than a god in their eyes."

Gemree looked again at the people thronging the narrow street that wound through the village. Every window, every doorway had bright eyes peering from it. The whole place was alive with waving hands and bubbling laughter. A power over which he had no control made him stop and dismount. Eager and willing hands grabbed Swiftsure's reins. He gave his hand to Tashka, and she slipped from her saddle. Together they walked down that long village street. Hands reached out to touch them. Eyes were filled with the tears that no emotion, other than that of love, coupled with the release of a long held fear, can produce. Gemree touched hands with crying women and smiling men, with happy and laughing children. Never in all of his life had he witnessed such happiness, never had he experienced such inner joy. In a flash of self knowledge he realized that, with these scenes in his heart and in his mind, the making of his sacrifice would be the easier. They reached the end of the long street. Gemree, together with a thousand pairs of willing hands, helped The Lady of Micrascar back onto Dark Star. With an easy action he swung himself up onto Swiftsure. At last the crowd was silent, and then a young boy stepped from within it holding a small stringed instrument. Cradling it in his arms, and picking at the strings, he began to sing in a pure and sweet voice.

"The Prince Gemree from Highworld came,
Twelfth knight of Orange and of Blue
He rode the waterfalls of death
To bring him to our world – the true
His destiny, if well fulfilled
Would save the lives of me and you ..."

The song went on to tell of the Plantmass, of Gemree's boat, the journey down the river, the fight with the huge bat, the bridging of the Pit of Snakes, the meeting with his Lady, his fight with Rantoc. It ended thus:-

"But now he rides, this Knight so brave,
To Slaco's gates, to pay the price
Of peace; in Arac's pleasant lands
He'll make that final sacrifice."

As the beautiful song drew to a close Gemree and Tashka wheeled their horses and rode onwards. She, a vision in white with her golden hair tumbling in profusion down her back. He, tall in the saddle, with his silver armour glinting in the sun under his bright tabard of orange and blue. his great broadsword, sheathed and hanging at his side. There they rode upon two magnificent animals that matched each other almost step for step. As they went, side by side, Gemree reached across and took the hand of the Lady. The village was silent. They knew, as the song had reminded them, that the Prince Gemree, Twelfth Knight of Arac, Knight of the Orange and Blue was riding to his final battle. Side by side, they watched them ride into legend.

Chapter 16

Slaco the Gatekeeper

Many days had passed since Gemree and Tashka had ridden from the village of Rantoc. Days that had passed like precious drops of water onto the desert's sand. As each moment had gone, Gemree knew it could never be recalled. That it was one moment closer to his sacrifice. One moment less to spend with his Lady. They had talked incessantly. They had talked of Arac and of Highworld. Gemree had told her of King Pylon, and of his brother Knights. Of Edmund, the first Knight of Arac, with his serious demeanour and his great skill. Of his deep love for all his brothers and the way, despite his own youth, he acted as father to them all. He told her of Fion, the eleventh and the youngest of the Knights. Fion with his boundless capacity for fun, of the endless jokes and tricks he played on his brothers. Of his constant smile, and the ever present warmth of his companionship. He told her of the twelve funny little squires on whom all the Knights depended so much, and, with a catch in his voice he told her of his own squire Pimm, his servant but his greatest friend. "I do miss the little fellow so much," he said. "I do hope he is well and that the fates protected him on the return from the mountains where I was forced to leave him." Tashka smiled, and her smile lit up the whole of Trueworld. As day followed day, Gemree thought, "If this is paradise, then let me spend eternity here." But he knew that that could never be.

One morning after they had risen and washed in the blue water of the river, the Lady had taken both of Gemree's hands in her own.

"My Lord Gemree," she had said. "These days we have spent together have been idyllic, and although they started as duty days for me, they soon ceased to be so." She stopped speaking and looked directly into Gemree's deep blue eyes before continuing. "My heart breaks at the thought that at the end of this day we must part for ever." Her voice caught. "At the end of this day – you will be dead." Gemree smiled and looked deeply into her eyes.

"Tashka," he spoke her name for the very first time, "do not weep for me. Such is my mission that I make my sacrifice willingly and with a light heart. I make it in the knowledge that my country, my King, my brother Knights and most of all the ordinary people of Arac, the men, the women and the children, people like those we met and left in Rantoc, will be safe." He paused. "When we walked through the village, when I looked in the faces of the women and watched the joy in the children, I thought – this could be the village where I was born, these could so easily be my own people. From that moment I have been able to face the future with calm."

"But my Lord, what of me? what of the Lady who now loves you more than life itself? Your death will be like my own, and I cannot bear it. Gemree, do you love me?" Gemree spoke softly. "Tashka, you are the most precious thing that has ever come into my life. I hear your laughter on the breeze. I see your eyes in the stars. I fall asleep to the sound of your voice, and I awake to the memory of your smile. Your beauty and your goodness has wrapped itself around me like a cloak that protects me from the world outside. I give a million blessings for these days that we have spent together. The pleasure of the memory of them makes my dying the easier." Gemree paused after his long speech, he looked down at the ground and was silent.

"If you love me my Lord, as you say you do, you will not go forward and give up your life. There is another course. We can turn away now, away from Slaco and the Great Gateway, away from your final ordeal. Together here in Trueworld, we could live our lives in paradise, in love and in happiness." She looked up, and her eyes were filled with tears.

"My Lady, do you love me?" although Gemree himself spoke softly, her whispered "Oh yes" was almost inaudible.

"Then you know that I cannot do what you ask of me. My honour as a Knight must be above all worldly things, as must my pride as a man. I have been chosen by a world which trusted that, whatever temptation fell my way I would not flinch from my duty. Although it will break my heart to leave you, I must, and I must face my death alone."

"Let us mount" said the Lady, "we will ride on together." But the magic had gone, for the first time since Rantoc they rode in silence. When the Lady did eventually speak, it was in a brisk and businesslike tone.

"Soon the river will flow into a lake. We will skirt its edge until it meets the foothills and then you will meet Slaco, keeper of the Gateway to Earthworld."

"My Lady," began Gemree earnestly "you must understand that ..."

"We must hurry my Lord," interrupted the Lady Micrascar, there is far to go." And so, as they rode on, silence fell upon them like a cloud. Gemree was desperate, although the sun still shone, the brightness had gone out of the day. He would have wished that his final hours could have been spent in deep and joyful conversation with the Lady who was most precious to him in all the three worlds. But she was withdrawn and offered no more than polite responses to his attempts at conversation. At last she stopped and put her hand on his arm.

"Gemree, listen to me carefully, I love you dearly but from now on I can help you no further. Around the next bend you will meet Slaco. May you face your death with great courage. Never forget, or doubt, my great love for you, and remember just this, things are not always as they seem." She leant across and kissed him lightly on the lips. Then, with tears in her eyes, she turned Dark Star's head, and galloped away in the direction from which they had come.

Gemree was devastated by the abruptness of their parting. He tried to call to her to return, but the words stuck in his throat. And then she was gone. With a heavy and sad heart he walked his horse forward. As he rounded the bend, he saw a sight that made him cry out involuntarily in shock and amazement. There, standing before him and blocking his path stood the Great Knight of Rantoc. The terrible drawbridge spikes still pierced his body, and he held his mighty war axe in both hands. Gemree heard Tashka's voice clearly in his head. "Remember Gemree, things are not always as they seem," and he thanked her for them. "Begone Rantoc, he called loudly, I have no desire to defeat you for a second time. I have watched your 'rolling on the ground' antics time enough, so begone." With a great laugh Rantoc disappeared, to be replaced by a small shrivelled being dressed in a bright green tunic.

"Good-day my Lord Gemree." He spoke in a clear, high-pitched voice, "I am Slaco, keeper of the Gateway to Earthworld, do you wish to pass through?"

"I do not Slaco" said Gemree, "I am here simply to open the Gateway for one who will follow me."

"Indeed," cooed Slaco, "Indeed you are, and do you know the price for opening the Gateway for your Follower?"

"I know the price, Slaco, the price is my life."

"And is your life a sacrifice that you are willing to give?" Slaco continued, "willingly, and without regret?"

"How can one give up a life without regret" said Gemree. "No, I give my life willingly to save my country. I give my life willingly in the name of honour. I give my life willingly, in the name of love. No Slaco, I do not give my life without regret."

"Have you no loved one," said Slaco " one who will perhaps grieve your passing?"

"I have a loved one," said Gemree "I pray that she understands."

"Then follow me my Prince – who am I to stand in the way of a life willingly given." Gemree dismounted and Swiftsure nuzzled his out-stretched hand. "Goodbye Swiftsure, you have been the finest friend a man could have. Go now, go back to my Lady, go back to Dark Star, they will care for you as I have done." Without a backward glance Gemree strode out to follow the small green figure who had scurried away in front of him. He seemed to walk into the mountain itself. Unflinchingly Gemree followed.

It was uncanny, as if the mountain was made of mist. They walked blindly on for some minutes only to suddenly appear in brightness again. Gemree looked out over a vision of total barren-ness. No trees, no grass, no water, just brown, dried, earth as far as the eye could see. Then, as they stood, out of the shimmering haze that hung over the ground appeared two huge gates, scrolled in black iron and standing in front of a dark back void. They stood higher even than those at the Castle of Rantoc. To each side of the great gates a pair of smaller, single gates, hung open, folded back into the blackness beyond. Above the left-hand gate was emblazoned in gold, the single word HONOUR. Above the right-hand gate the single word LOVE. But, joy of joys, framed in that austere gateway, her golden hair cascading over her shoulder stood his love, stood Tashka, the Lady of Micrascar. The smile, that so well remembered smile, lit up the day, and her eyes were bright with happiness.

"Come Gemree, through the gateway marked love and we can be together for always." Gemree covered his eyes and turned to Slaco. "What kind of trick is this?" he demanded. "It is no trick" replied Slaco, "Simply the truth, walk now through the gateway marked 'LOVE' and you can spend your eternity with your Lady, in happiness and joy."

"But, if I do so," said Gemree, "will the Gateway to Earthworld be unlocked"?

"If you choose the gateway marked LOVE, I will unlock the Gateway to Earthworld for seven days," said Slaco "plenty of time for The Follower to arrive."

"Do you know how far behind me the Follower travels?" said Gemree. Slaco smiled craftily.

"I am sure he is close," he said; "perhaps one day, perhaps eight; but surely it is worth that risk to spend eternity with your Lady?"

"What awaits me behind the gateway marked HONOUR?" asked Gemree.

"Beyond that gate lies your worst nightmares, one thousand Caverns of the Bat, one thousand Pits of Snakes, one thousand Great Knights of Rantoc. Behind that gate lies your death. Behind that gate there is pain followed by ... nothing. But, my Lord, the choice is yours, and yours alone."

"And if I choose HONOUR, for how long will the Gateway to Earthworld remain open?" Gemree asked.

"If you are foolish enough to choose Honour, then the Gateway to Earthworld will remain open until The Follower has passed safely through it, and it will re-open upon his request at his return" He smiled his evil grin once more. "If, that is, he does return."

Gemree looked again at his Lady, framed there in the Gateway of Love. "Gemree, please do not desert me," she begged of him. "If you leave me here I will die, can you really turn your back on my life, on our life together? Gemree, come to me now." She held her arms out towards him. "Come to me now." He gazed deeply into her eyes.

"I could not leave you to die, and I would give my life to save yours, but, my honour and my duty must come first. My Lady, both are bigger by far than our lives alone." He spoke now almost in a whisper. "Tashka, forgive me and understand, for I will love you for all time, and I will pray for your safe keeping." He turned to Slaco, "Gatekeeper, I take the gateway of HONOUR," and drawing his sword, and without a glance in either direction he strode forward into the blackness beyond. As he disappeared from sight, there was a loud crack, and the great iron and silver gates to Earthworld crashed open. And in that moment, Slaco, and the gates of HONOUR and LOVE, and Tashka, the Lady of Micrascar, vanished from sight.

Chapter 17

The Way of the Follower

Pimm and Donys looked around in wonderment. They were sitting on a sort of soft, green, spongy substance looking upwards at what appeared to be a million waterfalls. The water cascaded upon them with the colours of rainbows reflecting off the many-faceted sides of each water droplet. Although they did not know it, they were on the Plantmass in Trueworld. Just as the Prophesy had predicted, they were following the footsteps of Lord Gemree, the Twelfth Knight of Arac.

"Where do we go from here?" Donys asked, looking expectantly at Pimm.

"I don't know," replied Pimm, "but I do know that my master would have left nothing to chance for The Follower. I am sure that if we look around carefully we will find the answer to the next part of our journey." They stood up, and, just as Gemree had done before them, immediately sank deeply into the unresisting surface of the Plantmass. With the joy of youth they revelled in the experience, once, that is, they had discovered that it represented no danger. They fell about, backwards and forwards, sinking deeply into the soft, spongy greenness and laughing loudly. And then, by accident, Donys, who was getting nearer and nearer to the edge where the water splashed and ran swiftly by, discovered the strange little craft with the name "THE LORD GEMREE" carved proudly on the side. There was no doubt as to its purpose. Pimm laughed, and Donys clapped his hands excitedly.

"What fun, and what a splendid little boat," he shouted, "we must get in and trust to providence for our safety." Pimm chuckled. "No Donys, I think we can trust in Lord Gemree," and so saying jumped aboard. Donys followed him, and they sat there looking at the clever workmanship of the little craft that was about to become the vital ingredient of their important journey.

"There is no sail, nor any oars," observed Pimm, "so I suppose the river itself will take us to our destination, and so saying, he took the small knife that was always pushed in his belt, and cut the rope holding the little boat against the current. The moment the last strand parted, the boat was picked up by the swirling water, and sent spinning on its way downriver, with Pimm and Donys clinging to the sides for dear life. Like Gemree before them they soon realised that the small craft was impervious to the knocks and the bumps it received. They became quite confident that it was in fact quite unsinkable. Once they had accepted this view they were able to relax, and, sitting back soon began to enjoy the violent bumping motion as the boat sped over the tumbling water.

When Gemree had made his journey, his mind had been filled with the dread of the ordeals that lay ahead. No such thoughts crowded the mind of either Pimm or Donys. Both simply knew that Gemree would have cleared the way and ensured that no-where would danger await them. The thought that Gemree might have been defeated never even entered Pimm's head. His faith in his master's ability was absolute, there was neither man nor beast that could defeat Prince Gemree, the twelfth Knight of Arac in battle. It was therefore with an easy mind that he settled back and watched the eager excitement of Donys as they careered from one side of the river to the other. After some hours of this even Donys became bored with their predictable passage and began to complain of being hungry. It was a complaint that Pimm himself shared. Thirst was not a problem. Like Gemree, they had soon discovered the sweetness and clarity of the river over which they travelled. And the spray that constantly splashed over the boat's bow left them with no shortage. The thought of food had no sooner entered their heads, when their forward motion was suddenly arrested with such force that they were both thrown forward in a tangle of arms and legs to the front of the boat, which now seemed to be bouncing from side to side. Pimm could see from the rock face above him that in all other regards they were now stationary. As he peered over the side through the spray, the reason became obvious.

He saw a curious type of netting, just about three feet high. It stretched across the river from one side to the other at a point where the river narrowed between a high rocky outcrop and the Plantmass. Secured along this netting at intervals were tied bundles of the Plantmass, both root and plant, and a number of what appeared to be brushwood torches. Although unsure of their purpose, Pimm and Donys stood up and pulled the boat along the netting from one end to the other, untying the bundles and dropping them into the boat. Pimm was quite convinced that Gemree had left them there for The Follower to find -and then, on the last bundle was a short note that confirmed this belief. Written in a hand so familiar to Pimm it read:-

This fare is not a banquet and will appear strange to you, but eat with a will and you will not know hunger. The river's water is good to drink and you will not suffer thirst. I pledge to clear a safe path for my Follower. I will not fail you.

The Prince Gemree – Twelfth Knight of Arac.

The words brought tears to Pimm's eyes. As he read his masters words and realised that he would never see him again. "If only," he said to himself, "if only he could have known that I was chosen to be The Follower. Donys spoke, "Pimm, rest easy, I am sure that your Prince will know."

of all?" Donys did not answer, and Pimm climbed out of the boat and on to the bank where he tied the little craft to a low branch. He held out his hand to help the boy ashore but Donys made no attempt to take it, instead he stood up.

"No Pimm, my job is done. You have done well, but you must finish your journey alone. I had to know that you had reached the Gateway to the Earthworld safely. I had to know that Lord Gemree had succeeded in his ordeals and cleared the path for you to follow. Now I can help you no further; our world, our people depend on you and on you alone. Only you can pass through the Gate. Only you can find the Thirteenth Knight and bring him back to Arac. Only he can join the final Token that will seal the Secret Way for ever." He stopped speaking and Pimm stood, open mouthed.

"But Donys, what are you saying? You are only a kitchen boy, what can you know?" As Pimm spoke the words, 'only a kitchen boy' understanding began to dawn. Donys smiled, "Yes Pimm, I have always been 'only a kitchen boy', he untied the rope.

"Who are you"? said Pimm softly. The boat began to spin away from the bank against the current that had held it there.

"I am Donys, Pimm, your friend and your companion, just Donys." The boat was rapidly spinning out of sight. "Go now Pimm, find the Keeper of the Gate, and travel well, find the Thirteenth Knight and bring him back to save our land." The little boat was now almost out of sight, Pimm watched it go, and across the water he heard:

"I am just Donys – D.O.N.Y.S -Donys the Kitchen Boy." Pimm smiled as the truth struck him.

"Of course," he said aloud, "D.O.N.Y.S the kitchen boy. He carelessly traced the letters in the sandy earth, and then reversed them S.Y.N.O.D the most famous kitchen boy of all, the kitchen boy who became a King." With such a blessing how could he fail. With a whistling swagger he turned and marched straight through the great Iron and Silver Gate that stood open and facing him as he rounded the bend.

Pimm had been sitting on an upturned bucket by the side of the River Titchfield for a long time. A young boy approached him. His face looked vaguely familiar, but Pimm could not even remember who he was, so there was no chance of remembering a stranger.

"Ahem," said the young man, "is anything the matter?" Pimm ignored him, "perhaps he will go away and let me think" he thought. But he didn't.

"Ahem," he said, even louder "I said is anything the matter." And then all the exasperation boiled over.

"Of course – *everything's* the matter!" said Pimm, "I don't know where I am. I don't know who I am. I don't know where I came from. I don't know where I'm going to, and worst of all, I don't know how to get there … and oh," he added, "I am really rather hungry." The stranger looked at him with a kindly smile. "Well," he said, "You must come home with me and share my muffins."

Chapter 18

The Thirteenth Knight

Shout while you journey on
Songs be in every mouth
Lo, from the north we come,
From east and west and south

The trumpets had stopped their clarion calls, but now the drums had started to beat – slowly – every one of a million men matched their step to that insistent sound Not one drum. Not a hundred drums, but a thousand or more, insinuating their message deep into the minds of the marching men.

The ant-like column had heen threading its way into the dark mountain side for many days. A single file. One thousand men for every mile. Marching through one thousand miles of darkness. Through the very heart of a mountain range whose summits pierced the sky.

Before the journey was done, one million men of Sodah would be hidden from the sight of man. And then they would begin to pour out of the mountain, and into the green and pleasant land that was Arac.

Pimm's face was suddenly very serious. "Miss Colbran," he said, "I am very grateful to you for allowing me to join your class. However, I regret that I suddenly have business of a most pressing nature to attend to. I must ask you to excuse me, and indeed my Lord Gemree." He corrected himself quickly as the children began laughing again, "I mean Jeremy of course"

"Now Francis" said Miss Colbran, Sunday School is only for 60 minutes, just one hour every week. Surely it is not too much to ask you to give up your playing for such a short period." But Francis was most insistent.

"I am sorry Miss Colbran, but what Jeremy and I have to do really will not wait."

"If it is really so important Francis, then of course you may go" said Miss Colbran, "but I must insist that Jeremy stays until the end. I really could not let him leave without his mother's permission." Pimm bowed, a low bow, from the waist, which again had the children giggling.

"Please Miss Colbran, I do understand, and if you will forgive me, I will withdraw now and consider my problem whilst I await Jeremy's arrival." He turned to Jeremy. "Jeremy it is really very important that we talk."

Pimm dropped his voice to a whisper. "I have remembered who I am." He turned towards the door and then looked back over his shoulder. "I will wait for you at Colley's Bridge." When Jeremy arrived at the bridge, Pimm was seated on the stile that led to the meadow at the back of Apple Blossom Cottage. He was deep in thought.

"That was a funny exit Francis," said Jeremy,

you missed the story of Daniel and the Lions Den." Pimm looked up. "Jeremy he said, "the story I have to tell you now is stranger than any you have ever heard. Please sit next to me and listen carefully."

For the next hour Jeremy sat, open mouthed as he listened to Pimm's story. First he told him that his name was really Pimm. Then he told him of Highworld, and of the countries of Arac, Boldeg, Hanlon and Oblivia. He told him of the war with Sodah, and of the new perils now facing Arac, as the vast armies poured through the secret way beneath the mountains. He told him of King Synod, of King Pylon and the twelve Knights of Arac, and, of course, of his master Prince Gemree. He told him of Trueworld, and of the Visions and the Dreams. Of the Prophecy, and of Gemree's ordeals and his death. He told him of his role as The Follower, and his mission to journey to Earthworld to find the Thirteenth Knight.

"When," said Pimm as his remarkable story drew towards its end, "I passed through the Gateway to Earthworld, my memories left me. That is why you found me sitting on an upturned bucket not knowing who I was or what I was doing here. That is why, these many weeks of Earthworld time I have wasted the precious hours bought for me by my master's courage. It is only in the last few days that images have began to come back to me, and today, in the Sunday School, suddenly in a flash of light, I knew it all."

He paused before continuing and then looked Jeremy straight in his blue eyes. "You Jeremy, you are my Lord Gemree. I do not understand how, but you are his image in another world. I know, beyond all doubt, that you are the Thirteenth Knight, and in your hand alone, rests the salvation of my country and the safety of its people." He stopped speaking again. "Jeremy, will you return with me to Arac in the Highworld. Will you help me to fulfil my destiny, and ensure that Prince Gemree's sacrifice was not in vain. Will you help the eleven Knights to close the Secret Way for ever? I, my King, and my country are in your hands."

It was a long speech and Pimm closed his eyes, exhausted from the effort and from the painful memories. He sat silently awaiting Jeremy's answer. Jeremy was quiet for a long time. He was not a Knight, he was just a twelve-year old boy. It was true that he had his 'imaginations', and when immersed in them he might have been Ivanhoe, Sir Lancelot, or some other brave Knight. But that was, after all, only play-acting. In the middle of a battle he could always end a fight by shaking his head. If danger threatened, his mind could alter the rules and take it away again. What Francis, or should he say Pimm wanted him to do was to be a real Knight, in a real adventure. One that could be dangerous, one that could trap him in this Highworld, or worse still, in Trueworld for ever. What should he do?

"Francis," he said, you have told me an amazing

story that really frightens me. What if we are too late to close the Secret Way? What if I get stranded in one of your worlds? What of my family? It is a big decision you are asking me to make. I must have a few days to think about it."

"Jeremy, I know that what I ask you goes far beyond that which I have any right to do. But time is fast running out." He paused, and then said softly. "It may already be too late. My Lord Gemree has already given his life, I am my people's only hope. I was chosen to be The Follower, it was my destiny and I must not fail. But you took me into your home without question, and you have loved me like a brother. I cannot promise you that you will return safely to Earthworld and to your family, I cannot promise that you will even live through this great adventure. I can promise you honours in our land beyond measure if we succeed, and I can promise you the undying love of all my people. Most of all, my friend, I can promise you a place in our legends." He placed his hand on Jeremy's arm, "let us go now and have a last meal of muffins together, for tomorrow, together, or alone, I must return to report my success or my failure."

The moon was high in the sky when Jeremy quietly slid open the door to the garage where Pimm slept, and shook him awake.

"Francis," he said "I will come with you, together we will try to save Arac."

"Thank you my Lord," Pimm said simply, "but please, will you now call me Pimm. I am now, and must be your squire." Then he added with a smile, "and, of course, your friend." He stood up. "When can we leave?"

"I have left a note for my mother," said Jeremy, she will not understand it, but she will get it in the morning, I think it is better that we leave right away. Do you know the way to your Highworld?"

"No my Lord," said Pimm shrugging his shoulders, "but I believe it will be revealed to me if we start from the place that you found me all those weeks ago."

They left the cottage quietly and walked along the river's bank to Colley's Bridge. The wind, which had been blowing gently when they left the cottage now began to whistle more strongly, until, by the time they had reached the bridge it was howling loudly and whipping flecks of spray from the surface of the water. Pimm smiled gratefully at the all too familiar pattern. The two friends had to lean into the wind as they covered the final few yards. Jeremy was astounded to see, out of the corner of his eye, that small trees were now bending almost double from the violent onslaught of this wind that appeared to have come from nowhere. As they stood under the slight shelter of the bridge Pimm looked up and there in the middle of the river was the well-remembered Saddlestone. "Quickly," said Pimm, "we must reach The Saddlestone before the waters cover it completely." Without waiting for a response, he plunged into the deep, cold, water and struck out for the Saddlestone.

Without argument Jeremy followed him. The river was already running quite fast and it took all their strength to reach the safety of the rock. Once there it took only a moment for them to pull themselves safely out of the water. On their knees, they awaited developments. They were not long coming. Within moments the wind began to howl with a ferocity that Jeremy had never heard before. The water bubbled and crashed against the stone's sides. Thunder crashed as lightening lit up the scene around them.

"Lie down my Lord, and hold on to me, the Prophecy will do the rest." Never had Jeremy known such fury, as the wind and the rain beat against them. He was convinced that, had it not been for the slight protection that the bridge gave them, they would have been washed off into the now raging torrent that used to be the gentle River Titchfield. He looked up, despite the flashes of lightening, the world that he used to know so well now appeared to be just a black void. The bridge had gone, and the lights of the village, which had been twinkling in the distance were no longer visible. The air was filled with a noise that cracked the ear drums.

"Rest easy my Lord," shouted Pimm, "it will soon be over." And so it was. Slowly the great winds calmed. The thunder's crash became softer and then stopped. The lightning's urgent brightness faded away to nothing. And the rain, which had been beating a violent tattoo upon the world, became a gentle drizzle, and then stopped altogether.

Pimm stood up and looked around him. He recognised the formation of boulders and the shape of the black pool in which The Saddlestone now lay. He knew he was back at the source of the River Titch. The point from where his journey to Earthworld had begun. Jeremy had also risen. He became aware of a bright glow over his shoulder and he turned. The sight that met his eyes was as magnificent as it was heartwarming. Standing on a high flat rock was King Pylon, a truly majestic sight in his ermine edged warrior's robe. A robe of deep crimson with a broad golden belt from which hung his great war sword. Slightly below him on the banks of the pool, sitting ramrod straight on the backs of their magnificent horses, were eleven young men, resplendent in their silver armour with tabards of brightly coloured silk. Every one had removed his plumed helmet and these rested on the saddles in front of them, revealing their extreme youth, and the pride in that youth that shone from their eager eyes. Holding the horse's reins were eleven little fellows, and each one of them looked exactly like dear Pimm. In their hands they each held a flaming torch, and these were the source of the brightness that lit up the night sky. Pimm bowed low from the waist towards King Pylon, and there was a loud cheer from the company of Knights and their squires, with calls of, "Well-done Pimm!" "Welcome back Pimm!" "A Hero's cheer for Pimm"! The little man stood there beside Jeremy, wreathed in smiles at these accolades. Jeremy felt a lump begin to rise in his own throat as he saw the tears of happiness begin to well up in Pimm's big black eyes.

King Pylon lifted his arms high, and the Knights and Squires fell silent.

"My Knights," said the King, "We have a thousand thanks to give, and as many questions to ask our dear friend Pimm and his young companion. But first, do you think we should do them the honour of removing them from their precarious perch and giving them a dry robe to warm them?" Almost before he had finished speaking two of the young men had spurred their horses forward, and plunged into the cold deep pool. In seconds the first had swum alongside The Saddlestone and Jeremy found himself looking into the bright blue eyes of a young man barely three years older than himself. As he looked at the young man, he saw in his eyes a look of great shock and disbelief, and for a moment his smile fell away. But only for a moment, and then he had recovered himself, and holding out his arm he spoke.

"My Friend, please take my hand, I am Edmund, the First Knight of Arac. May I be the first to thank you for your courage in coming here to try to save our beautiful land." Jeremy looked hard at the young man. So young to hold such an exalted position. A position that was his by birthright, as was each of the other Knights. He smiled back warmly. He just could not believe that this was really happening to him. It was infinitely better than his very best 'imagining'. So much more exciting than his most exciting dream. It took just a moment before both Pimm and Jeremy stood on the bank and the Knights, having dismounted clustered around to greet them. There were great bear hugs for Pimm, and warm sincere handshakes for Jeremy. Time and again, as a Knight took Jeremy's hand and looked into his eyes, Jeremy was struck by the strange reaction. A clouding-over of the eyes, and the temporary fading of the broad smile, as if in disbelief. It was but a fleeting moment, and then the handshake tightened with great warmth, and the smile returned more broadly and more welcoming than before. Some of them even changed their greeting to a curious. "Welcome home, my dear friend." It was not until Fion, the eleventh Knight stood before him that the mystery was revealed. He stood there, and, like the others, his mouth dropped open in amazement.

He did not offer his hand, but instead, put his arms around Jeremy and hugged him tightly to him saying – "Gemree, my dear friend and brother, you have survived, the Prophecy said that you would die. Welcome home my dear dear friend."

After the Knights the little squires all filed past Jeremy and, shaking his hand and politely bowing, offered quiet but sincere words of welcome. The night that followed became so special that Jeremy knew that it would live in his heart and mind all his days. The little squires scurried around and quickly built a huge fire of brushwood and branches. Then the King, the eleven Knights and the eleven little squires sat in a huge circle around the fires warm glow. Jeremy sat on the King's right hand and Pimm at his left. That night Jeremy heard such wonderful stories. But the most wonderful of all was that of Lord Gemree, the Twelfth Knight, the Knight of the Orange and Blue, the youngest of all the Knights and certainly the most loved. It was as the stories about the brave young man unfolded, and the incredible likeness between the two of them explained, that Jeremy began to fully understand the re-action of the other Knights, particularly those of Fion, when they first saw him.

"It is true," said King Pylon when Jeremy had asked if he really so resembled Gemree. "You are the very image of our dear lost friend. We do not begin to understand how one with such a likeness, who even shares so close a name, could live a quite separate life in a different world. But, whatever the reason for so great a mystery, there is no doubt that you are The Thirteenth Knight, promised by our Prophecy. It is you who have been chosen by a power outside of our understanding.

They did not sleep that night, and as the sun rose King Pylon stood up and addressed the company.

"For two full cycles of the moon," he said, "the hoards of Sodah have been pouring through the hidden opening to the secret way of legend. Now more than one million men draw close to our land. We know only that they will emerge at a point close to our sacred Tablestone, and it is upon the Tablestone that our Tokens, all twelve, must be joined with the Trueword whose secret you each hold. The Prophecy says that if just one man of Sodah reaches the sacred Tablestone, the Secret Way can never be closed and our land will be ruled forever. We know not how close they draw to the hidden entrance, but must now move with great speed and pray that we are not too late. King Pylon swung himself into the saddle of his great charger. The little squires were pulled up to sit behind their Knights, and with a single command of "Forward!" they set off at a canter towards the place where the Tablestone lay.

It had taken twelve days to reach the Tablestone, and, since daylight the eleven Knights had been busying themselves at their tasks. Now it was almost dusk. Throughout the long day a deep throbbing sound had chilled their bones for they knew that it came from the marching feet of a million men. A column of destruction that wound its way through the mountain, ever closer to the entrance that would pour them on to Arac's soil. The sound had been growing louder with each hour that passed. Now it filled the air as well as their minds. Dusk was falling as King Pylon called the Knights to him. "My Princes," he started, "I am not yet one quarter through the preparations that the Prophecy demands before the Tokens can be joined. I fear that the men of Sodah will be spilling on to our land long before they are complete. If they do so, they must not reach the sacred Tablestone, and I charge each of you with the duty to prevent it. If one man of Sodah touches our sacred stone, the Secret Way will be open for a million men to overrun the country we hold so dear. Edmund," King Pylon spoke directly to the first Knight, "I had hoped that you and your bothers, who have borne so much, would be spared this final battle. Sadly I fear that is no longer so. We must make our plans."

And so, for a second night, the company of Knights sat around a warming fire and talked until dawn, for only in the light could the preparations continue. "You are but eleven" said Pylon "your enemy will number by the hundreds and then the thousands, but still you can buy the time that we need to join the Tokens." He turned directly to Edmund. "The entrance is wide enough for just two men at a time. You must deploy your brothers skilfully. Deal with each man as he appears, but remember, each of you must lay his own Token on the Tablestone and speak the Trueword. Each must be correctly laid by its brother, and when all twelve Tokens are laid, twelve hands must be linked and the final ritual spoken. That is when we will be unprotected and most vulnerable. Eleven against so many is formidable odds."

"Sire" Pimm's soft voice cut across the night air, "we are not eleven, but twenty-three, I know that I speak for all my brother squires when I say that we will fight, and die if needs be, to protect our land, and our King," Pylon smiled,

"I will not argue against you Pimm, nor would I doubt your courage, you have proved that a thousand times. So be it, let there be twenty-three."

"Twenty-four Sire." Jeremy hardly realised that he had spoken until the words had been said, "I am strong and fit, and although untrained, let me try to fill the place left by my namesake. let me make it twenty-four."

"So be it," said the King "and thank you. Now Edmund, deploy your men."

The mountain began to rise some 1000 yards or so from where the Tablestone lay; the ground between was littered with small clumps of barbed desert scrubs. To the right was a small lake, filled from a stream which tumbled down the mountain's sloping side. The entrance to the Secret Way lay almost hidden in a fold of perpendicular rock.

At a height of some ten feet above the entrance, the mountain began to slope gently away with its surface covered with shale and small loose rocks. The cavern entrance itself was indeed so narrow that two men could barely squeeze by each other. However, the distance from the ground to the arched roof was at least four times the height of a man. Edmund gathered his Knights, the squires and Jeremy together and outlined his plan.

THE THIRTEENTH KNIGHT

"My brother Knights," he said, his arm indicating not just the eleven, but the twelve little squires, and Jeremy as well. "listen to the drums. Our enemies are close, and our duty is clear. Not one must reach the sacred Stone." He paused, and then began to pace up and down. "Yet our duty goes still further." For a long time he was silent, as if conceiving his plan, then he began to speak rapidly.

"Our fight is secondary to the joining of the Tokens," he said, "and so we must ensure that the ritual can be fulfilled." He drew his sword and with its point he drew a straight line on the dusty ground. "This," he said looking up, "is the mountain, and here," he drew a cross in the centre of the line, "is the cavern's entrance. To the right is the lake, and to the left open, and therefore dangerous land. Here," he drew a square directly opposite the mountain's entrance, "here is the Tablestone. Now, the Tokens must be placed in strict order, from the First Knight: myself, down to the Twelfth Knight: our dear Gemree, whose Token is now carried by Pimm. Finally our new and special friend, our brave companion, Jeremy, must join the twelve Tokens with that of the Thirteenth Knight, and the Trueword." He paused and looked around. "This is what we must do."

First, I want the squires to climb up to the slopes above the cavern's entrance, and," he looked at Jeremy, "Jeremy, I would like you to be with them. From that vantage point, my friends, you can render invaluable service to us by raining missiles down upon the heads of the enemy if, and only if mind, it seems that we might be overcome. And now my brother Knights, our foes will come from the mountain just two by two, and so that is how we will meet them. At the beginning, the entrance will be guarded by you Fion, and Mala, Knights ten and eleven. You are the last who will be required at the Tablestone. Ten yards from you will stand Luan and you Erac, the eighth and ninth Knights, and so on in two's. Ten yards between each pair. I will take station closest to the Tablestone. When I have placed my Token I will replace the eleventh Knight, and the second Knight will go to the Tablestone to place his Token. So on until all Tokens are laid, with each Knight covering for his brother. And now my brothers and my friends, take your stations, and let us prepare for battle."

Chapter 19

The Final Battle

Clear before them in the darkness
Gleamed and burned the torches bright
Brother clasped the hand of brother
Stepping fearless through the night

As the fragrant sweetness of dawn slowly pushed away the shadows of the night, eleven young men, twelve strange little beings, and the boy from Earthworld prepared for whatever this day would bring. As the light revealed the mountain's entrance Prince Edmund's voice rang out in a long forgotten prayer. A Knights prayer, as old as Synod himself:

"Teach us to fight, that we might dread
The grave as little as our bed
And if today we die – we'll ride
To dwell victorious at Synod's side."

The Knights knelt down and the words of a barely remembered response fell from their lips,

"Redeem our mis-spent time, that's past,
May we live this day, as if our last."

And then, as if that 'Knights Prayer' was the signal, the drums that had, as the night had progressed, reached a crescendo, fell silent. In that moment, an all pervading quietness filled the early day. Suddenly, Fion, the eleventh Knight, stood up and raising his sword motioned to the other Knights to be silent and ready themselves. He had caught just the barest glimpse of movement inside the entrance.

Slowly and silently he crept forward until he stood to the left of the entrance with his back pressed hard against the granite wall. The other Knights quickly drew themselves sideways so that they were not in the immediate line of sight. Suddenly, like a swimmer seeing the surface of the water when his lungs are about to burst, a figure exploded joyfully out of the blackness of the mountain's interior and into the bright sunlight: the first he had seen for many days. He was a dozen steps from the cave's entrance before he looked up and found himself looking straight into the blue eyes of Mala, the tenth Knight. He turned and rushed back towards the safety of the mountain, but he had no chance, as he turned Fion stepped forward, and struck him down with the hilt of his own sword. Three more men had followed the route of their comrade. Three more men had been struck down before one fellow, more cautious than the rest, peered out carefully from within to survey the scene. He spotted the still bodies of his fallen comrades, and then the waiting Knights. Almost immediately his head vanished back into the darkness. Fion, still standing close to the entrance, could hear hurried whispering from within, but could glean nothing from it as it was in a tongue that he did not understand. He knew however, that the narrowness of the passage prevented two men from standing side by side, and the whispered messages of this development were obviously being passed back down the line.

Now that its head had stopped, the whole column, which stretched many miles back into the mountain, had come to a halt. After a while Fion heard the clatter of horses' hooves. The men were obviously squeezing themselves tightly against the mountain walls while horses were being brought forward to the entrance. For some while there was silence, and then the same face appeared again. It looked quickly to the right and left, and then withdrew. Fion re-acted quickly, and motioned all the Knights forward so that they formed a wall just 20 yards or so from the entrance. He realized that if the Knights remained in their present positions, the horse would have time to break into a gallop and would soon be unstoppable and thus capable of carrying its rider to the sacred Tablestone. Their only hope lay in unseating the man before the horse had time to get into its stride. Because of the narrowness of the entrance, horse and rider now emerged slowly, and the Knights were able to move forward in challenge. As soon as the horse was clear the Knights formed a circle around it and it was a matter of moments before the rider was on the ground. He jumped to his feet quickly, but although he fought gallantly, he really had little chance against the Knights and was soon overpowered. Edmund stepped forward and slapped the horse on the rump with the flat of his sword sending him cantering harmlessly away. The now familiar face re-appeared, took stock of the situation, and vanished from sight again. Twice more a horse and rider appeared, twice more the result was the same. No further horses appeared, and for a long time nothing happened, whilst the men inside wrestled with the fact that, despite their far superior numbers, they appeared to be helpless against the small band of young men who awaited them.

The next move had, to some extent, been predicted by young Edmund who was proving himself to be a worthy leader. Inside the cave the waiting men had obviously lined up in two's with the intention of quickly following each other from the cave to engage the Knights in battle. Clearly their hope was, that whilst the Knights were so occupied, their comrades would have time to leave the mountain unmolested. The ploy almost worked. The first two men rushed out and, although they knew that their action could have but one end, they threw themselves upon the waiting Knights. They fought with great ferocity and courage before they were cut down. By this time however, at least a dozen men had, unchallenged, been able to escape from the cave and join their comrades. Edmund realised, that unless he could staunch this increasing flow from the mountain, his comrades would soon be overcome. Tapping Fion on the shoulder, he led the way at a run, back to the cave's entrance where they were soon crossing swords with the small group who had, or were in the process of forcing themselves out of the mountain. This fight soon began to go against them and they were driven back away from the entrance, thus allowing others to leave. The other ten Knights who had fought valiantly against almost twice their number, were gradually getting the upper hand, and, in ones and two's, they were able to fall back to try to staunch the flow from the mountain's side.

For over an hour the battle had raged, and although they were able to strike down man after man, there was always another to take his place. Miraculously, the dribble from the mountain had been contained and not allowed to become a flood. But by now the Knights were tiring, while the new men joining the battle were fresh and untried. Edmund realised to his dismay that they were beginning to lose the conflict. His men needed a moment's respite if they were not to be overcome. It was time to try a new means of attack. He drew back and looked up to the mountain slopes above the cave entrance, hoping that Pimm and Jeremy had used their time well. He quickly saw that they had not been idle.

Jeremy had sized up the situation quickly, and had instructed the squires to cut a number of branches from the small stunted trees that abounded on the mountain's slopes. He had had two of these branches securely driven into the ground on the slope almost immediately above the point where the men of Sodah were emerging from the mountain. Between these two branches he had interwoven others to make an effective barrier. He had then sent the little fellows scurrying about hither and yon, collecting armfuls of small rocks. These he had placed behind his makeshift barrier until it was bulging with their weight. Edmund could see that Jeremy had tied a rope around one of the uprights and it needed no more than a tug upon this rope to send a whole avalanche of rocks crashing down upon the men below. Jeremy looked down, and seeing Edmund's upturned face waved cheerfully. Edmund blessed his new friend's cleverness and signalled to him to make ready to send the rock pile tumbling down. All the Knights were now being hard pressed as more and more men were managing to squeeze out of the mountain and into the battle.

Edmund gave the signal for the Knights to break off the fight and to retreat on the run. As he did so, the Knights stopped abruptly and turning sprinted away from the astonished enemy, who took a moment to gather their thoughts. Believing that the opponents were beaten, they let out a cry of victory and began to run after the retreating figures. Edmund stopped and turned, and raising his sword signalled to Jeremy to release the rocks. He was relieved to see that already Jeremy had all twelve squires holding onto the rope like a tug-of-war team. The moment he saw Edmund's upraised sword he yelled at them to "Pull with all your strength." Battle excitement lent them strength and the upright branch leapt from the ground. In an instant the barrier collapsed under the weight of rocks that began to roll down the short mountain slope before crashing over the edge onto the men below. Some of the men of Sodah heard the rumble, and looking up saw the danger. They were the lucky ones who were able to dart to right or left to get out of harm's way. Most of them, particularly those men still squeezing out of the cave's entrance, had little or no chance. For some minutes the crashing of the rocks mingled with the cries of pain of the men who vainly held up their shields to protect themselves. At last it was quiet. The Knights turned, and even they were appalled at what they saw. A group of some forty to fifty men had escaped injury completely. They stood dumbstruck at the way the victory they had moments before believed to be within their grasp, had been turned into disaster. Men still moaned quietly beneath the pile of rocks. Arms and legs could be seen twisted and bent in unnatural actions. But, the greatest shock of all for the men, now on the outside, was the fact that of the cave's entrance there was now no sign, other than a small gap some fifteen feet or so above the ground and beyond the top of the pile of rocks.

THE FINAL BATTLE

From Jeremy's point of view the success of his action had succeeded all expectations. The falling rocks had caused others to slide and tumble from the mountain, multiplying ten-fold the pile that he and the little fellows had prepared. As they realised the success of their actions the Knights let out a great cheer, a cheer so loud that King Pylon, who for many hours had been immersed in his own world of ritual preparations, looked up. Seeing the huge rock pile covering the entrance, he called loudly, "Well done my Knights, well done," before once more bending to his task.

Up on the mountain slopes the little fellows were jumping up and down with joy, hugging each other, dancing around in circles, and slapping each other on the back. Jeremy just stood, smiling proudly, and accepting eveyone's praise with a huge grin, and very little modesty. Down below, Edmund was quickly assessing the situation and preparing for the next assault. The eleven Knights were still faced with some forty to fifty men-at-arms, and their position was far from secure. Although, thankfully, no more men would be able to join the fray, the Knights were, by this time, very tired and still substantially outnumbered. Added to their opponent's natural desire to be victorious, there was now a deep anger at what had happened to their comrades.

The man who had kept popping his head in and out of the cave earlier in the morning, stood at the head of this angry band. He was clearly an officer and had proved himself to be an able leader. He now acted in an unpredictable way which underlined that view. He was faced with a choice. He could immediately dispatch all of his men against the eleven Knights in the hope of quickly overpowering them, thus bringing the whole affair to an end; or he could detail a part of his remaining group to try to clear the mountain entrance and simply hold the Knights at bay until the way was clear for his temporarily entombed comrades to join him. He chose the latter course, and detached a full dozen men and set them to work clearing the rocks that blocked the cave's entrance. Only time would tell if his decision was the right one. The remaining men, who still numbered more than thirty, began to advance upon Edmund and his brothers.

Edmund too had spotted the choice that lay in the officer's gift, and it was not one he would have liked to have made. It was obvious that the entrance could not be cleared from the inside, as with the entrance being only wide enough for one man the task of dismantling the whole mountain would have been no more difficult. Clearly the entrance had to be cleared from the outside. The gamble that the man had taken was a simple one. Could thirty men, if not defeat the Knights, at least delay them long enough for the job to be accomplished? Edmund suspected that either choice put the advantage massively with the men of Sodah, but there was little to be gained from this line of thought. So, with a cheerful call he rallied his brothers, and at a run, they took the battle to the enemy.

Their initial attack was met with a wall of resistance that stopped them dead in their tracks. Most of the Knights were having to defend against at least two swords at once, and it took all their skill not to give ground, let alone to make significant headway against the Sodah's wall of steel. However, they had their minor victories, and after half an hour or so, all eleven Knights still stood, even though a number of their opponents had been struck down. Jeremy and Pimm had noticed, with some dismay, that the dozen men working on the rock pile were now beginning to make substantial inroads. Miraculously, there also appeared to be a number of men who had been partially buried by the avalanche and had sustained no serious injury. These men were now adding their hands to the task.

Jeremy realised that unless he took a hand, it would not be too long before Edmund and his brother Knights were overrun. He sent a number of the squires running up the slopes once more to gather as many small rocks and stones as they could carry.

These they brought back to Jeremy and the remaining squires who stood waiting, overlooking the men below. At his signal they began to rain these tiny missiles down upon the heads of those working so industriously on the rock pile. Whilst they had little chance of inflicting serious injury, this hail of rocks was a great annoyance, and quite capable of causing some pain. Certainly it disturbed the well established work pattern. Within a few moments their progress had slowed significantly as they tried to protect themselves with upraised shields. It did not take the leader long to realize that he had to take some positive action. He called six or seven men away from the battle with the Knights, and had them stand around the rocks with their arms upraised, a shield in each hand. This formed a very effective 'roof' over the working men, and despite the efforts of Jeremy, Pimm and the others, very few of their missiles were now having any real effect. The work rate on the rock pile was, although still well below the original, markedly improved. However, with the men who had been struck down by the Knights, and now a further six or so withdrawn for other works, Edmund and his brothers were able to take new heart. At last they were beginning to beat their opponents further and further back towards the mountain and away from the Tablestone. They were careful always to keep themselves between the two so that no man could make a break and try to cover the distance to the sacred stone before he was brought down.

It was now that King Pylon sent Pimm, who had returned to his side after the avalanche, to tell Edmund that at last the preparations were complete and it was time for the joining of the Tokens. Out of the corner of his eye, Edmund saw Pimm approaching with his familiar lopsided little run. Guessing the reason, he allowed his opponent to drive him backwards a little so that he was on the edge of the battle and Pimm would not be required to run the gauntlet between flashing blades. His original plan of spacing the Knights so that each was ready for the placing of his token was now in tatters. As he looked around at his brothers, all deeply immersed in the concentration necessary to fulfil their tasks and stay alive, he knew that he would have to place a great and dangerous burden on the brave little squire.

Just in front of him, Fion had successfully struck down the man he was fighting, and looking around he saw that Edmund was fighting alone, with Pimm by his side. Quickly grasping the meaning of Pimm's presence, he stepped to Edmund's side, and took the fight away from Edmund and onto himself. Edmund smiled his gratitude, and taking Pimm out of danger's way spoke quickly to him.

"Pimm," he said "time grows very short, I have a task for you that is important and dangerous – I know I can rely upon you," and he quickly told him what was required of him. When Edmund reached the sacred Tablestone, King Pylon was looking anxiously at the scene by the mountain's face.

"Edmund," he whispered, "how goes the battle? Edmund told him of Jeremy's cleverness, and how, thanks to that and the skill of his Knights, they were holding on, for the moment."

"But," he continued, "each minute the pile gets smaller and I fear it will not be long before the entrance is open again and then we will be overwhelmed." Pimm by this time had returned and stood next to Edmund, waiting to take his sword when the time came for him to lay his token.

"Pimm," said the King, "go to the Knight's horses and take their bows, and ten arrows. Lay them out on the ground in a line, just within range of the mountain's entrance, then go to Jeremy and tell him to judge when his usefulness above the entrance is at an end. At that moment tell him to send the squires, each to take up station by his Knight's bow and to fire upon the men as they emerge from the cave." The King paused and his final comments were almost spoken to himself. "Perhaps that final obstacle will give us the time we need. Go now, and good luck."

He then turned to Edmund. "Well my Prince, we now come to the most difficult part of the ritual which I have prepared according to the Prophesy. Each Knight must now lay his Token and speak the Secret Word, the word given to him by King Synod himself, the word that he alone knows. I know not how the Tokens fit, but there is but one way that they make a whole. Each Knight must take great care for there will be no second chance. And now Edmund, commence the joining which marks the end of the Prophecy for which we have journeyed so far."

Edmund took from his tunic a small triangle of smooth, black rock. He laid it upon the flat surface of the sacred Tablestone, saying as he did so – "I am Edmund, The First Knight of Arac, Knight of the Black, I lay my Token" he looked hopelessly at the flat, bare and unhelpful expanse of the Tablestone. "I lay my Token to scourge the Evil of the Word – and the Word is BAT-CAVERN." As he said the Word and laid his Token on the Tablestone, there was a great crash like thunder and a sheet of fire like a bolt of lightning. The Token lay untouched, but burned into the Tablestone was its image, ten times its size and across its centre emblazoned in gold the one word BATCAVERN. Edmund, still kneeling picked up his sword. Placing the hilt in front of his face, he bowed to the Tablestone before standing and racing back towards the battle.

Pimm had done his work, for half way he met Prince Fannon, the second Knight. Fannon arrived at the Tablestone and King Pylon spoke to him just as he had to Edmund. Fannon took his Token, somewhat larger than Edmund's, and triangular, with a base of a far more irregular shape. The Token was of a deep blue crystal. Fannon looked down as it lay in his hand. He looked at the small black triangle that Edmund had already placed on the Tablestone, and he smiled with relief. From their respective shapes there was clearly only one place in which his token could lie. He leaned forward.

"I am Fannon, Second Knight of Arac, Knight of the Blue and Black, I lay my Token in the name of Good. I lay my Token in the name of "DARK

STAR." Again, the flash of light. Again the crash of sound, and when they were done, two Tokens, Edmund's half moon and Fannons larger triangle, fused together as one. Their joint image burned deeply into the Tablestone, with the words, BATCAVERN – DARK STAR etched side by side.

One by one the Knights laid their Tokens.

"I am Ogam, Third Knight, Knight of the Green, My Token is laid in 'Evils' name – THE PIT."

"I am Hanno, Fourth Knight, Knight of the Yellow and Green, my Token is laid for Good in the name of MICRASCAR."

"I am Retne, Fifth Knight, Knight of the Purple, my Token is laid in Evils name – RANTOC."

As each Knight laid his Token, first a half moon in the name of Evil and then a triangle in the name of Good, so the flame flashed and the thunder crashed and the Tokens first fused together, and then, burned a larger image upon the sacred Stone.

"I am Smadra, Sixth Knight, Knight of the Blue, I lay my Token in the name of Good in the name of SACRIFICE."

"I am Tevdu, Seventh Knight, Knight of the Red, I lay my Token in Evils name, the name is FALSELOVE."

"I am Erac, Eighth Knight, Knight of the Green and Red, I lay my Token in the name of Good in the name of SYNOD."

"I am Luan, Ninth Knight, Knight of the Yellow, I lay my Token in of Evils name, the name is SLACO."

THE FINAL BATTLE

"I am Mala, Tenth Knight, Knight of the Black and Yellow, I lay my Token in the name of Good, in the name of DONYS."

"I am Fion, the Eleventh Knight, Knight of the Blue, I lay my token in Evils name, the name is PLANTMASS."

By now the cave's entrance was almost clear. Despite the fact that, for much of the past 30 minutes or so there had always been two Knights effectively out of the fray, the superior skill added to their youth and fitness had ensured that they had stayed well in command. However, notwithstanding this fact, they had been unable, at any time to take a position whereby they could prevent the progress at the rock pile. Now it was clear that it would be but a matter of moments before men would start pouring from the mountain to join their comrades.

Throughout the whole battle Pimm had been a marvel, running from Knight to Knight with his familiar little lopsided run. He had warned them when it was their turn to lay their Tokens on the Tablestone. He had watched eagerly as the Knight had completed his ritual, and as soon as he saw him pick up his sword to return to the battle he had warned the next Knight to be ready. In between, he had retrieved the Knights bows and arrows and laid them at a place, slightly sheltered, but within range of the mountain entrance. He had rushed up the mountain slope to give Jeremy the King's message and to tell him about the bows.

THE THIRTEENTH KNIGHT

He had rushed from Knight to Knight shouting encouragement as the ritual drew closer and closer to its end. Pimm turned towards the Table-stone and seeing Fion, the Eleventh Knight, picking up his sword, automatically prepared to warn the Twelfth Knight. So wound up was he in the events of the day, that for some while he had forgotten that the Twelfth Knight – his own dear Prince, the Lord Gemree was dead, and that he, Pimm, held his Token and the Word. He turned towards the Tablestone and ambled off as fast as his little legs would allow him. When he arrived, King Pylon smiled his encouragement. Pimm dug deep into the folds of his tunic and pulled out the Token that Gemree had given to him in what seemed a lifetime ago, high in the Mountains of Synod. He tried desperately to remember the words he had to say, but his mind was completely blank. He looked in panic at the old King, who, understanding his torment whispered softly.

"Pimm, proceed with your Token, the words will come, believe me, the words will come." Pimm looked down at the flat surface which was now almost completely covered by a huge Star within a Circle, burnt deep into the stone. A star with six points, each point bearing a single word in gold. Between the points a name in silver. On the edge of the Tablestone was a smaller raised star, and Pimm realised that this was formed by eleven tokens like his own.

There was one place that his token could fit, and leaning forward he prepared to place it there. As he did so, the words flooded into his mind. With relief he looked up at the King, only to find that he was not watching Pimm, but was instead, staring in horror at a point over his head. Pimm turned and looked over his shoulder, and in so doing saw the very sight that they had striven to avoid. Men were now pouring out of the mountain and beginning to converge upon the Knights.

Pimm lost not a moment. Thrusting his Token back into his tunic, he leapt off the Tablestone and rushed across the open ground to where the eleven squires were kneeling, frozen with terror at the awful sight before them. Pimm picked up the first bow and notching an arrow into its string he sent it flying across space, where, as great luck and providence would have it, it found its mark in a soldier's thigh sending him crashing to the ground. Pimm thrust the bow into the squire's hands shouting, "keep firing, Lom, keep firing, we are our King's only hope," and rushed on down the line. He picked up bow after bow, notching an arrow into its string and firing at the mountain's face before passing it into the quivering hands of the waiting squire. "Elcab, Midian, Harib, aim your arrows, we cannot let down our King," he shouted, as he moved from one to the other. In just a matter of moments all eleven little fellows had shaken off their terror and were firing arrow after rapid arrow. Their aim was poor, and often the arrow's flight had barely enough strength to reach the mountain wall, but once again the flood was stemmed. The mountain, for the moment gave up no more foes as those in the open tried to find cover from the rain of sharp tipped missiles falling from the sky. Pimm, his work done, raced back to the Tablestone, pulling his token from his tunic as he ran. He fell upon it saying: -

"My name is Pimm, I am The Follower. I act for my master the Lord Gemree, Twelfth Knight of Arac, Knight of the Orange and Blue. I act in the name of he who gave his willing sacrifice for his brothers. I lay his Token in the name of Good, I lay his token in the name of THE LADY TASHKA."

This time the crashing of thunder was so loud and the flash of light so bright, that momentarily everyone stopped, even in the heat of their battle, and turned towards its source. At the Tablestone Pimm looked with wonder as the final Tokens welded together, and the image was burned into the surface of the Tablestone in a perfect star. A star with a circular hollow in its centre, a hollow that awaited the Thirteenth Token, the Token held by The Thirteenth Knight. But where was Jeremy? Pimm looked desperately around. What he saw made him recoil in horror. The little squires were still busy firing flights of arrows at the mountain entrance. From what Pimm could see, most of the arrows were off course, but although the pile of arrows by the bows were rapidly diminishing, the little men seemed to be achieving their objective. No-one else had appeared to join the soldiers locked in mortal combat with the young Knights.

However, the Knights themselves were, by this time, being extremely hard pressed. Tired from several hours of fighting with hardly any respite, they were now having great difficulty in holding the men; at least double their number, who fought them. Both of these sights gave Pimm great cause for concern. He knew that somehow, the eleven Knights, Jeremy, and himself, had to form a human circle as Jeremy laid the last Token. He could not see how the Knights could possibly break off the fight, and reach the Tablestone with enough time for the ritual to be performed, before the men-at arms had fallen upon them. And then he saw Jeremy, and cried out loud at the sight before him. Still on the slope above the cave's entrance, Jeremy was crouched, half hidden between two large boulders. A large bearded man, his sword flashing from side to side, was trying desperately to reach him. Although Pimm knew that without Jeremy, the Tokens could not be joined, that was not the first thought that flashed into his head. As he took in the scene and imagined its probable end, his only thought was that Jeremy, the dear friend who had given him muffins and called him Francis Drake, was in terrible danger. At that moment, there was nothing in the three worlds more important than that he, Pimm, should save him. For what seemed the thousandth time that day the brave little fellow set off across that unfriendly battlefield as fast as his lopsided little run would carry him. On his way he picked up

Lord Gemree's bow which still lay on the ground where he had dropped it, and from where the other little squires were still madly firing their dwindling supply of arrows at the mountain. He ran until he was as close to Jeremy's huge antagonist as time permitted, and falling to one knee, notched a single arrow to the bowstring.

Jeremy had looked down on the frightful scene below. He knew, beyond doubt, that if many more men joined those fighting the violent battle with the brave young Knights, then the result would be in no doubt. Even though the crumpled bodies of many of the enemy lay on the rocky floor, and all eleven of the Knights still stood, Jeremy could see that a number of his new friends were obviously hurt. It was hard to believe that the blood that streaked their faces did not include a fair proportion of their own. He decided that the number of rocks now available as missiles made their continued efforts pointless, and sent the squires slipping and sliding down the slope and running across the open ground to the place where their master's bows had been left in readiness. He watched them go on their way, and then put a final plan of his own into operation.

Close to the point where they had conducted their battle Jeremy had noiced a large, almost round boulder that was standing beside another similar in shape, and appeared to be balancing precariously. He wondered if, with a little help, he could send it crashing down the mountainside. Grabbing a long branch that had formed part of the barrier for the piles of rocks, he had raced over to the boulder. Standing between them he had placed the branch underneath and was straining with all his might. The boulder was beginning to creak ominously when a shadow was cast over his face. He looked up. To his horror he saw standing over him a huge bearded man, his sword raised high in the air and in the act of slicing down in an arc which Jeremy knew would take his head from his body. There was no time to do anything at all, and Jeremy, frozen to the spot, waited for the blow to land. Suddenly a most extraordinary thing happened. The sword was already down to shoulder level when the man's eyes suddenly became glazed and unseeing. His mouth silently fell open. The sword fell from his hand and hit the ground, followed closely by the man himself. The man's arm had fallen across Jeremy and he struggled to push it out of the way and stand up, still unable to believe his good fortune. As he stood, he found himself looking into the beaming moon-round face of that dearest of friends, Pimm. He began to walk towards him with his arms outstretched.

"My dear friend," he said, "you have saved my life."

Pimm didn't answer, but his mouth fell open in sudden astonishment, and his big black eyes opened wide with surprise. As Jeremy reached forward to hug him to him, he fell forward into his arms. It was then that Jeremy saw the lethal black arrow sticking out from between his shoulder blades. He looked down at the scene below him and watched the eleven little squires still madly notching arrows to their master's bows. They were firing wildly at the cave's entrance – unaware of the devastating effect of one apparently wild shot.

"My Lord," said Pimm, his eyes bright with pain, "It is time to join your Token, please hurry to the Tablestone or we will be too late." Jeremy almost cried out at the hidden truth of Pimm's words. Picking the little fellow up carefully in his arms, he set off at a steady run towards King Pylon and the Sacred Stone. On the way he stopped at the place where the little squires were busy about their work. Some of them caught their breaths as they saw Pimm in his arms, still with the cruel arrow sticking out of his back, but Jeremy quickly silenced them.

"Hod," said Jeremy recognising one of the squires, "go to your master, tell him it is time for the Knights to return to the Tablestone. Tell him they must break off the battle swiftly and together, and to run as if the wind is on their heels. He turned to the other squires. "And all of you, the moment there is a space between your masters and the enemy you must change your fire, away from the cave and prevent them from following to the sacred Stone. Go, now Hod. With these words he turned and continued his own race towards where the King still stood. He reached the Tablestone and laid Pimm gently at the Kings feet.

"Pimm is badly hurt sire, call the Knights, there is no time to lose if the Tokens are to be joined." Jeremy knew nothing of the Tokens. Nothing of the Prophecy. Nothing of the Trueword, and yet in that single moment he knew it all, and he took charge.

"Sire, summon the Knights, Hod has told them what to do," and as the King turned towards the fighting Knights, Jeremy, who now, in some miraculous way, knew all there was to be known, took the curious little circle of bronze from around his neck. He looked up. The King with arms upraised had called out just one word, "Edmund." He had not shouted the word, and yet it had carried across the rocky distance. It had cut through the sounds of steel on steel, like a word spoken in the stillness of the night. Edmund, that remarkable young man, had known exactly what to do, he had motioned to his companions to break off the fight. At his word they had turned and run with great speed showing their backs to a surprised enemy. A gap of more than twenty yards had opened up before they had realised what had happened. Before they could give chase, a hail of arrows had cascaded among them sending many to the ground. The little squires had performed their task well, and had loosed a second flight into the enemy's confusion.

The Knights had reached the Tablestone. Jeremy was now in complete charge, although his words and his actions came from he knew not where.

"King Pylon, quickly, stand within the circle, here, by my side," – he motioned. "My Lords, stand each of you in front of your own Token's mark, and link hands." He carefully lifted Pimm until he stood before his master's Token, between the Fion and Edmund, the eleventh and the first Knights

"Edmund, Fion," he said, "Support our dear friend, for the circle must be complete." He looked into Pimm's large sad eyes, the little fellow bravely tried to smile although it was clear that he was in great pain. Jeremy looked around, the circle was complete with himself and King Pylon standing within it. He took his medallion, and placed it in the hollow centre of the Star, already in it's place.

"I am Jeremy of Earthworld. I am the Thirteenth Knight summoned by Pimm 'The Follower' after the willing sacrifice of the bravest Knight in the Three Worlds. I place my Token, given to me by the Stranger in Earthworld, in the name of Good. I place my Token for the Lord Gemree and in the name of HONOUR."

There followed the same bright flash, the same crash, as of thunder, and then the image burned into the Tablestone as the Tokens welded together to form one complete star. And then the wind began to howl as Jeremy, with his eyes closed, continued to speak.

"These tokens here before us laid
Are for the Prophecy true made,
Six points are Evil overcome,
Six points march well to honour's drum
We join our hands and recognise,
Honour – and Gemree's sacrifice,
Now close the Secret Way – close tight,
I ask this as, The Thirteenth Knight."

The wind reached fever pitch – it was a wind such as Jeremy had never heard before, on his journey with Pimm to the Highworld. There was a great crescendo of sound and then, suddenly, there was calm.

Jeremy came to slowly, as if from a trance. He remembered all that had happened, but could not remember the words he had spoken, nor the marvellous source from which his knowledge had come. King Pylon was on his knees, his eyes were closed, his lips were silently moving, as if in prayer. The Knights cautiously let go of each other's hands and laughed nervously as they looked around.

Edmund and Filon gently laid Pimm on the Tablestone – his eyes were closed, but he smiled as he slept. The face of the mountain was of smooth unbroken rock for as far as the eye could see. The crumpled bodies of several dozen men, lying among the discarded swords and shields were the only evidence of what had been. Except, that is, for eleven funny little fellows who were sitting around, unhurt, but thoroughly bewildered, clutching hard onto the bows and arrows, which legend would one day declare played such an important part in that day's events. King Pylon opened his eyes.

"My Princes, my brave, brave Knights, and of course, our clever little squires." He turned and swept his arm sideways to encompass the little men, who were now getting to their feet and beginning to amble over to where the others stood. "We have succeeded, the Secret Way is closed. You have all been magnificent, just like the Prophecy said you would be. But our special thanks must go to three very special people." He paused and looked around the tired, but contented faces. "To Lord Gemree, The Twelfth Knight, who met Ordeals, the horror of which we will never know, and who, when his courage had been tested to the utmost, willingly gave us his life."

"To our new and dear friend Jeremy, who fate and the Prophecy has brought to us. Jeremy, the Thirteenth Knight, who knew nothing of our world, but left his own with no guarantee of a safe return so that he could help us."

The King smiled gratefully at Jeremy before he continued. "And to the bravest of them all. To he who became The Follower. Who, untrained, and with only his great courage, and even greater heart, travelled through unknown worlds to undertake an impossible task; to find the Thirteenth Knight. To him who this day has been everywhere as warrior and leader, as messenger and as saviour. Yes indeed, to the bravest of them all …"

"Sire." King Pylon stopped speaking and turned at the sound of Jeremy's voice. He was kneeling over the still form of the little squire. "Sire," Jeremy repeated, and then, with tears in his eyes and a lump in his throat, he looked up. "Pimm is dead."

EPILOGUE

The homecoming should have been a time of great joy. But it was not. The death of Pimm hung over the company like a great black storm cloud.

Although there were banquets and fireworks; athough there was dancing in the streets, and honours bestowed and received; the happiness that should have been felt by the the Knights and their squires was absent. Their faces smiled their appreciation but the smile was not in their eyes, nor the pleasure in their hearts. Although they felt deeply the death of their brother Gemree, it had been a distant death. Their memories were of the tall, vital young man with the easy smile and caring ways. But, of Pimm, they were different. Their memory of him was of a dear little fellow mis-cast. An honest, brave and caring squire, carrying out duties well beyond his calling, and doing so with a kind of courage that brought tears to the eyes. As The Follower, undertaking a journey through unknown worlds, the hope of a a whole people resting upon his narrow shoulders. As the little warrior, rushing around the battlefield on that final day, with his funny, lopsided, little run. Never flinching from the dangers that surrounded him. They saw him again, willing his comrades on. Kneeling, with bow in hand showing them the way. They saw him in his final act of sacrifice racing to protect Jeremy from a giant of a man with destruction in his heart. They saw him fighting the pain as he willed himself to live until the Tokens had been joined, and his people saved. They saw him lying dead upon the sacred Tablestone. Dead, at the very moment of triumph. These were the visions that filled their hearts. These were the visions that left no room for happiness.

They had laid Pimm to rest beneath the sacred Tablestone, but his story had journeyed before them to the cities and the towns throughout the land. He was hailed a hero and honoured above all others in every household; but there was not a Knight or a squire who resented it. They too were honoured and revered throughout the land, but it was of Pimm that the people spoke.

Jeremy, an unlikely hero, did find his way, with the help of others, back to Gramblehampton in his own world. The journey was not easy, but that is another story. He took with him memories of dear friends and of an adventure so exciting that none of his 'imaginings' were ever the same again. People would ask him where Francis Drake had gone, and he would smile sadly, and say simply, "Francis? oh, he has gone back home." As time passed, and memories faded, he would take from under his pillow a wonderful Star within a circle. A star of the strangest and most beautiful stone. In its centre a curious bronze medallion. Within the segments of the star, emblazoned in gold, were strange words. MICRASCAR, PLANTMASS, RANTOC, TASHKA and many more. Meaningless to everyone, except of course, Jeremy himself.

It was this Star of Tokens that was to open the 'Door of Time' for Jeremy. A door through which he was to make many journeys in the years that followed.

As The Lord Gemree had turned away from the gate marked LOVE, away from his Lady – still framed in its portals, he had unsheathed his sword. In the full knowledge of the horrors that awaited him, he had strode bravely through the gateway marked HONOUR. He had glanced neither right nor left as he stepped from the light, into the black void of nothingness that lay beyond He was barely conscious of the flash of light or crash of thunder that followed his entrance, but his heart almost stopped at the vision that confronted him as he passed through that barrier of blackness. In front of him lay the most beautiful vision in the Three Worlds. He was back beyond the mountains. He was back in the meadows of Micrascar, and there sitting on the river's bank carelessly throwing petals into the gently flowing blue waters, just as she had been when he had frst seen her, was his Lady herself. Swiftsure and Dark Star grazed contentedly nearby.

"My Lord," she said, rising, "My dear brave Knight. Welcome to paradise, to our eternity together." Gemree started to speak but Tashka placed her fingers on his lips to quieten him.

"Hush," she said, "I will explain. You must forgive me for the trickery I was forced to play, but the Prophecy demanded that you were tested to the utmost. I was the instrument chosen for that test."

She smiled sadly at him, "I prayed that you would not weaken. I prayed that when I told you that all was not what it seemed, you would understand. But you were steadfast, you chose the Gateway of Honour and earned your paradise."

"What then awaited me through the Gateway of Love through which you tried to tempt me?" Gemree asked the question, though he feared her answer.

"Through that Gateway, my Lord, would have been all the nightmares promised to you by Slaco, the Gatekeeper. Nightmares, pain, death and then an eternity of nothingness. But you chose honour. Your part in the Prophecy is now over my Lord, your reward is here and now. An eternity where time has no meaning.

The Lord Gemree rode by the side of Tashka, his Lady, in the land of perpetual sunshine that was Trueworld He was happy, and yet his life was not complete. In the days since he had walked through the Gateway of Honour, he had known only joy and peace. Yet his heart, which now shared love in abundance, missed the essence of friendship that had been his life.

On this day, as he rode, he looked pensively towards the hills. He thought he saw movement among the rocks, and he strained his eyes to catch a further glimpse. He reached down, and grasping the reins of Dark Star, he spurred Swiftsure into a canter and started towards the place.

As he got closer, a small figure emerged, scrambling from between two round boulders. A funny little figure, with silver buckled shoes and a doublet of orange and black He looked up and saw the Knight and the Lady riding towards him, and with a great big grin, and a funny little lopsided run, he started ambling towards them.

The Thirteenth Knight
Competition Entry Form

I have read the story of 'The Thirteenth Knight', and I
know the name of the Ninth Knight of Arac.

The name of the Ninth Knight is

....

Name...
Address...
....Post Code ....
Telephone ....

Please Complete and Return to:
Octopus Distribution Limited,
Arnside House,
32 Hutchinson Square,
Douglas, Isle of Man.

The prize, which is ongoing will be announced in July
and December each year, commencing in December
1996